Ray wondered if there was something special about Jana that was ...him.

She was certai... number of oth... them had mad... she said or done any...ing that set her apart from all others?

Yet when he closed his eyes, he could still see her there on the hospital bed, her arm around her little son who'd been so very ill, even in sleep cuddling, holding, loving him. Had something that simple, that basic, brought into focus Ray's own need for closeness?

He wanted to be with Jana, to talk with her, to get to know her for who she really was—not only as an excellent student and loving mother, but apparently a good friend to the other young mothers she'd lived with. And her appreciation of and love for her Gram was also in her favor.

Ray couldn't sort out his thoughts. For someone who prided himself on his clear thinking, on being able to concentrate on whatever he chose and push from his consciousness things that would interfere, this was almost intolerable!

Books by Eileen Berger

Love Inspired

A Family for Andi #57
A Special Kind of Family #132
A Family for Jana #160

EILEEN BERGER

has always loved fiction, and even as a teen promised herself that she'd someday write a novel. However, that had to be put on hold as she earned degrees from Bucknell and Temple Universities, then headed up a pathology laboratory in Michigan.

She later married Bob, whom she'd known since childhood, and moved back to north central Pennsylvania, only about twenty miles from where they'd grown up. She did then write several novels, which didn't sell, although hundreds of articles, short stories and poems were published. It was only in the nineties that her first novels were published—and the one in your hands now is number thirteen.

Eileen is active in writing circles, especially St. Davids Christian Writers Association, whose excellent annual conference is the second oldest and one of the most prestigious of those in America, and possibly in the world.

She says that without these wonderful, caring writers, instructors, co-workers and friends, her career as a Christian writer would have been not only less successful, but much more lonely.

A Family for Jana

Eileen Berger

Love Inspired®

Published by Steeple Hill Books™

STEEPLE HILL BOOKS

ISBN 0-373-87167-8

A FAMILY FOR JANA

Printed in U.S.A.

Dear friends, let us love one another,
for love comes from God and knows God.

—*I John* 4:7

This book is dedicated
to
our blessed grandsons,
Nathanael,
Isaac,
Samuel
and
Karl,
with many prayers and much love,
from your
Grandmother.

Chapter One

Jana Jenson felt heat rising up her neck and face. She'd heard titters, which called her wandering thoughts back from the hospital; looking toward the front of the college classroom, she realized that Professor Hawkins was staring at her, right eyebrow raised quizzically. "I'm sorry, Dr. Hawkins, did you—ask me something?"

"Yes, I did, Miss Jenson, and...."

She knew better than to interrupt, but it seemed necessary to explain. "My three-year-old son was very sick during the night, and I had to take him to the hospital. My mind was with him, wondering how he's doing without me there in the pediatric department."

There was a moment's silence, but she was looking at her college embryology textbook, fighting for composure. She felt a hand on her shoulder, squeezing it, and heard the encouraging voice of Todd Livingston, who was sitting behind her. "I'm sorry, Jana—we all are."

She nodded to show she'd heard and raised her left hand to cover his for a moment in nonverbal thanks. Linda, on her left, asked, "What's wrong? What happened?"

Jana risked a glance at the professor, not knowing if he'd be offended if she continued, but others were also asking questions. "Michael's been having increasingly bad attacks of croup during this past year. I usually get it under control by filling the bathroom with steam and sitting there with him as the medicine takes effect, but last night even that didn't bring relief."

She swallowed the unshed tears, which felt as though they were about to choke her. "I finally called nine-one-one, and the paramedics came—and took him by ambulance...." She was still not over the panic, the fear of losing this child for whom she'd already given up so much—her baby, for whom she'd gladly give her life.

"Is he all right now?" Todd asked.

Jana wished she could be sure of that. "He was some better when I left him—" she glanced at her watch "—about forty minutes ago. He's no longer critical, they tell me. Otherwise—" she looked directly at Dr. Hawkins "—I'll admit that I would not be here today."

His expression had changed, and he looked as though about to respond, but Linda was asking, "How will you manage when he gets home again? Do you have your mother—or someone?"

This question she could readily answer. "Gram will take care of things." But no, Jana wouldn't go into further details concerning what she owed that wonderful woman who, though not a blood relative, had done so much for her. Gram had far more than filled the void in her life when she was forced to leave home because of dis-obeying her parents' command. *And I have no regrets as to having made that decision!*

She tried to force herself to pay close attention to the rest of the lecture. *Meiosis*. It was un-doubtedly a fascinating subject, and she really did want to learn more about the study of which one of each pair of homologous chromosomes goes to each daughter cell. However, as troubled as she was, Jana couldn't fully concentrate on the lecture.

Class was finally over, and Todd and Linda waited as Jana gathered her things. However, as they passed the large, centrally located front table, Dr. Hawkins asked, "May I please speak with you, Jana?"

That was the first time he'd called her by her given name. Glancing toward her companions, who nodded and left, she hugged her books close to her chest. "Of course."

Taking a couple steps around the table, he looked into her eyes and said, "I would like to apologize for embarrassing you."

She wasn't convinced he was sorry but would try to give him the benefit of the doubt. "It's all right."

Perhaps he sensed her reservations. "I should have just gone on with the class, not waited for you to respond."

She met his gaze. "I may be setting myself up for an F, Professor, but—" *I shouldn't be saying this—I need good marks to keep my scholarship* "—I believe you sometimes enjoy playing to your audience."

His eyelids flickered, then steadied, and she

clutched her books closer, sure she'd made a major error in saying that. But then what appeared to be a rueful smile twisted his lips. "Ah, you are a courageous one, Jana Jenson—but I assure you that, though I may be guilty of sometimes playing to my audience, as you so succinctly put it, I *never* penalize someone for having the courage to speak the truth. There are few who would take that risk."

His smile seemed to become more sincere, and his right hand cupped her left elbow. "I promise to try doing better—and hereby give permission for you to hold me accountable if I slip up."

She started to relax, and her responding smile felt as genuine as his now looked. Continuing to hold her books in her left arm, she impulsively thrust out her other hand. "I will cheerfully accept that responsibility, Dr. Hawkins."

His grip was firm, and he started to say something else, but she'd glanced at the wall clock, appalled. "Oh, no! I must call the hospital before going to my other class this morning! I'm going to be late."

He lightly tugged the hand he was still holding as he headed for the door. "My office is right

down this hallway. You might as well call from
there."

Todd and Linda were waiting outside, their
concerned looks changing to puzzlement, then relief as Jana said, "Dr. Hawkins offered the use
of his office phone so I can call the hospital. If
Michael's okay, I'll run over to Richards Hall for
my next class."

Linda nodded. "Any chance of making the
noon meeting?"

"Not today." She shook her head. "Perhaps
tomorrow, if he's a whole lot better."

"You have meetings each day?" the professor
asked as they walked rapidly down the hall.

He was probably just making conversation, but
she could, too. "It's available each noon, but I
usually make it only once or twice a week."

"*Noon* meetings?"

"Uh-huh. The Christian Association has done
this for years."

"What do—?" But he interrupted himself by
inserting the key he'd taken from his pocket,
opening the door, turning on the light and indicating the desk phone. "It's all yours."

It took only moments to get through to the
pediatric department and learn that Michael was

asleep. He appeared to be better, although he was still coughing and wheezing some—but that was to be expected, she was told.

"He's apparently doing okay, and sleeping right now," she told the man beside her as she replaced the phone. She drew in a deep breath, let it out slowly, then relaxed a bit. "It's so scary, especially at night—which is when it almost always happens. I'm grateful that he's healthy otherwise, and active. Once he's over even a serious attack, he quickly bounces back."

"I'm glad."

"And I must dash!" She was outside the room as she called over her shoulder, "Thanks for the use of your phone."

Raymond Hawkins stood in his doorway watching the hodgepodge of students, like Jana, rushing to get to their next class. She hurried through the exterior door of the building, and through the glass making up the far side of the covered passageway he saw her leap over the border of blooming tulips and daffodils and run across the grass to save a few seconds.

Only when the door to Richards Hall closed behind her did he turn back to his own office, shut the door, lean back against it—and catch himself sighing. He knew nothing about Jana Jenson—well, almost nothing. He'd noticed that she was not wearing a wedding ring but, until a few minutes ago, had no idea she was the mother of a three-year-old.

And she had guts!

He'd been too aware of her from that very first day in his class. She was incredibly beautiful, with those wide, intense, dark blue eyes and slightly wavy hair the color of that well-pulled brown sugar-taffy he and his sister used to help their mother make each year between Thanksgiving and Christmas.

How long has it been since I've thought of doing that—or of eating it? Is it because of her speaking so lovingly of Gram, who would help care for little Michael?

He started going over test papers from the morning's first class, an advanced one on the human endocrine system, and was pleased that most students were doing well. That class and the one just ended were his favorite courses, partly because of his personal interest, but also because they were electives, so the students taking them were those with a genuine interest in the subjects.

He'd known he would have to mostly teach required subjects for at least the first years of his career. This was his fourth year—since those in power agreed to count that first one, when he'd taken over in early October for a professor who had a massive heart attack. These two courses he'd asked for two years later were something of a reward, he thought, and they made such a difference!

Jana must be older than she looks—or else she had her child when very young. He was surprised to realize his thoughts had reverted to her—and was almost glad when the phone rang and he had to take care of some detailed information. That was much safer than continuing to think of that gorgeous junior. Or might she be only a sophomore?

He did wonder about her. No, she was definitely not wearing a ring on her left hand—and she had a three-year-old son.

And she was evidently a Christian....

Jana slid into the empty seat immediately inside the doorway and, grateful to find the class just beginning, quickly opened her notebook. Statistics. She'd taken it because she thought she should, but was discovering she liked it. *Whether I use my early-childhood education degree in a school or some other institution, understanding these principles and problems could be invaluable.*

Her mind kept wandering; she so wanted to be with Michael, to hold him and sing to him and calm him if he was frightened or lonely. She did manage to drag her thoughts back fairly quickly each time—but it was taking more and more effort to squelch her eagerness to leave.

Class was eventually over, and she drove to the hospital to find Michael no longer lying listlessly against the high-tilted mattress. He was sitting up in bed, and his face became one big smile. "Mama, you're back!"

"Yes, sweetie, I sure am, and I plan to stay." She made sure he saw her place her books on his dresser before going to him. "I came as quickly as I possibly could."

She pulled away as he shoved a small stuffed raccoon into her face. "Look, Mama, Aunt Vanessa brought him, and his name is Raccie."

She hugged and kissed Michael, which also gave her the opportunity to make sure he didn't have an elevated temperature along with his wheezing. "That's a perfect name for him! Did you think of it all by yourself?"

"Uh-huh," he said, beaming with pride. "I think lots of things all by myself."

Her knuckles brushed lightly along his jawline. "You certainly do, and that makes me happy." After lowering the side rail, she sat on the side of his bed. "And now I want to hear all about your morning—what you saw and who you talked with and everything."

He rattled on about the nurses, a funny TV cartoon, his Aunt Vanessa, who was actually Gram's granddaughter, the raccoon and Gram's phoning while Vanessa was there, saying she'd be coming soon. Jana encouraged his enthusiastic report, rejoicing in his communication skills even while being very aware of his continuing cough and breathing difficulties.

At least neither was as bad as before.

It was some time later that she stood up and, walking toward the door, laid her hand on the books. "I'm leaving my stuff here, Michael, while I go down the hall to talk with one of the nurses."

His little arms reached toward her. "Don't go, Mama."

"I'll be right back, dear."

His face began to pucker. "Stay with me."

She wanted to gather him into her arms, but instead stood there smiling, praying that her manner and voice would reassure him. "I promise to come back very, very soon, Michael."

A tear formed in each eye. "Last time was a long time."

"I know, Michael—but remember I told you then that I must go to school and I would be gone quite a while—and I was. And *this* time I'm saying it will be just a *little* while, okay?"

His lower lip protruded, but she grinned, quickly walked over to put up the bed rail and left immediately, saying cheerfully, "See you in a tiny little bit, my love."

She did not turn back when he cried, "Mama, come back, come back!" She leaned against the wall and waited to make sure his starting to cough harder didn't make his wheezing more serious.

"Something wrong, Miss Jenson?" It was one of the older cleaning ladies. "Something wrong with that dear little boy of yours?"

Maybe I'm what's wrong. Jana glanced at the woman's name tag before whispering, "I just got back from my classes, Sandra, and need to speak with Michael's nurse—but he doesn't want me to leave.''

A big smile covered the woman's round face, and her hand on Jana's waist gave a light shove. ''We talked a whole lot while I was cleaning his room, so I'm gonna go in there and visit with that little cutie. We'll make out fine.'' She then walked inside, saying, ''Hi, Michael. What have you and Raccie been doing since I left?''

Jana smiled with relief as she heard her son answer the question. *There are so many wonderful people in Your world, God! Thanks for letting me get to know that—for letting me know them. And help me not to forget to help others....*

She spoke first with the secretary, and was even more grateful for Sandra's being with Michael as she waited several minutes to talk with the nurse. Margery Caldwell appeared harried, but did say that Michael was doing ''as well as can be expected at this time.'' Nobody had any idea yet when he might go home, certainly not today—but she assured Jana he was over the worst of the attack.

When Jana returned to Michael's room, Sandra bent over to kiss his cheek. ''See, big guy? Your mom's returned real quick, like she said—and now I'd better get back to my job before I get in trouble.'' On the way to the door she took time to add, ''And you, Ms. Jenson, don't worry so much. We're here to help take care of your little boy.''

''Thanks, Sandra.'' Jana reached out to squeeze her hand. ''You have no idea how comforting it is to know that.'' She put down the side rail and sat on Michael's bed again as she told him the nurse said he was better.

''Yep.'' He nodded. ''Better.''

She touched his chest. ''Does it hurt here?''

He shook his head. ''Nope.''

''*Did* it hurt?''

''Yep.''

''Where did you hurt?''

''Here!'' His fingertips beat a brief tattoo on his chest, then moved to his throat. ''And here.''

The wheezing. And coughing. ''Well, since they're both better now, would you like to get out of bed?''

He was instantly slithering around her, legs already over the edge of the bed as she grabbed him. ''Michael, wait a second! Look down there—how far it is to the floor. This is a high bed, not like yours at home with its short legs.''

She convinced him to sit while she got his pajamas and bunny slippers from the bag she'd brought with her. ''And as soon as you go to the bathroom, and change out of that gown and into these clothes, we'll walk in the hall.''

He was so overjoyed at this prospect that it was difficult to keep him still long enough to slide his legs into the pants and his feet into slippers. She held him as he tugged to run down the hallway. Remembering how very sick he'd been during the night, she wasn't sure how much energy he should be expending.

At the end of the corridor, she lifted him so he could look out the window. ''What do you see, Michael?''

''Oh, trees and grass and sidewalks and men and women and cars and streets and a dog....'' It was a singsong reply, with all nouns emphasized. ''And clouds and shadows and birds and branches—I see *lots* of things.''

''Yes, dear, you certainly do see lots of things, and I'm glad you showed them to me. I had not even noticed those shadows.'' After all, she and Michael were on the fourth floor.

"Lots of shadows—the big, *big* one's from the ho'pital, and the littler ones are from trees—but it's hard seein' people shadows."

It seems to me that these are astute observations my three-year-old is making, but what do I know? Until he was born, I hadn't been around many babies and small children.

They took their time walking to his room, for he had to investigate a wheelchair and climb on it. She pushed him a short distance before returning it to where it had been, and then they proceeded to his room. She let him press the button to raise the top of the bed and, after removing his slippers and her shoes, she lay down beside him to read several of his favorite books. It wasn't long before his eyelids were getting heavy, but she made no comment about this, just kept on reading until he was sound asleep.

The rail was still up on the other side of the bed, and she hesitated to lower it in case that might awaken him, or might even make him worse. Laying the book on the bedside table, she turned onto her side with her arm around him and closed her eyes. *I should use this time for studying, but I'm exhausted. I'm going to rest a few minutes....*

* * *

Ray Hawkins was not used to making amends—most times he'd found it wasn't necessary, particularly now that he was a tenured professor at a well-rated institution. However, though Jana Jenson had indicated that she'd accepted his apology, he still didn't feel good about what he'd done to necessitate it.

Well, he'd discovered for himself the truth of the florists' ads—that a dozen long-stemmed roses or some seasonal arrangement did seem to please women. He reached for the phone and started to dial that remembered number—but stopped in time.

There was a good possibility that this particular woman would not only see through his sending flowers, but tell him so!

Like she'd done after his class!

Well, then, he'd send flowers to her son; that shouldn't offend her. He checked with the hospital for the child's room number before calling the florist to order something suitable for a three-year-old in some clever pot or vase that a little kid would like.

Feeling pleased with himself after his phone conversation, he returned to looking over the material for tomorrow's classes then, not bothering with lunch, finished checking over the tests from yesterday. He'd asked only one essay question in addition to all those requiring an answer of a few words, so the task was completed in less time than anticipated.

Picking up his briefcase and suit jacket, Ray left his office for the day, locked the door and went to his car.

On the spur of the moment he stopped at the florist's to check the arrangement he'd ordered— and was annoyed when told that whichever container and flowers might be used, it wouldn't be delivered until tomorrow!

Among the assortment of glass, ceramic and pottery containers, one in particular appealed to him. He'd been a railroad buff for as long as he could remember, his particular interest being steam engines. For the last ten years, ever since he was nineteen, he'd belonged to one, then another railroad club. His present one had not only restored an old station house, but also was in the continuing process of revamping an engine, caboose and various cars.

There was no doubt about it—this little steam engine with its burly black bear engineer and antlered-deer fireman was what he wanted for Michael. And it was after making that decision he belatedly recalled that some croup attacks were triggered by certain flowers or strong scents—so what he'd already ordered could be dangerous.

He carried the ceramic engine to the counter and informed the clerk that instead of flowers he wanted small plants in this container, and he'd wait for it to be made up so he could take it to the hospital himself.

The counter person stated she was too busy to do that right now, but he reminded her that she'd not told him on the phone his order wouldn't be delivered today. Since he'd have to deliver it himself, he'd just borrow the stool from behind the counter and wait until his order was taken care of.

Seating himself in the busiest part of the shop, he began reading the professional journal that had come the day before, and it was no surprise that his order was made up quickly. He carried it to his car, then headed for the hospital, realizing that even though he should be rooting for the child to already be well enough to go home, he couldn't help selfishly hoping Michael was still there—and that his mother was with him.

The hospital parking lot was almost full, but

someone was pulling out of a spot near the entrance, so he slid into that. He seldom went to hospitals because he found them depressing, but this time he didn't think of that. He did, however, wonder what in the world he could talk about with a child this young—or with anyone else, for that matter—if Jana wasn't there. How could he explain to a stranger his personally bringing a gift for this child he'd never met?

He forced himself to get on the elevator when the doors opened—but had there not been people awaiting the exit of whoever pushed the button for the fourth floor, he might have stayed on for a return to the lobby to hand this planter to someone at the front desk. As it was, he stepped into the hallway and stood there for a moment, unsure where to go.

A cheerful older woman wearing a volunteer name tag caught his eye. "Can I help you?"

"Yes, please. Room four fourteen…?"

She pointed toward his right. "Make a left at the end of this corridor. It's the third door on the right."

"Thanks." But his steps were slow as he followed her instructions. The partially open door showed only the foot of the bed, but as he stepped inside he saw first Jana's stockinged feet, then legs that were quite worthy of notice! Then there was the blue-and-beige skirt and beige blouse Jana had been wearing this morning—and that lovely oval face.

She was lying on her right side, facing him, arm around a little boy with the same fair skin and sugar-taffy hair. His breathing sounded raspy, but Ray had never just stood and watched a sleeping child. He supposed this might not be too abnormal, though it seemed that the little chest, as observed through the cotton pajamas, was rising and lowering more than he'd have expected. Was it perhaps overfilling—perhaps needing more oxygen than usual?

It occurred to him that, notwithstanding all his studies in biology and human anatomy and physiology, in spite of his degrees and being one of the youngest tenured professors on campus, he knew very little as to three-year-olds—and was intrigued by the possibility of learning more about Michael.

As he already was about the child's mother.

Ray had, of course, dated through the years, but always tried to keep from developing more than a short-term relationship. After all, his goal had been to get where he was now—so why wasn't he more contented and fulfilled? Why did he have this something driving him to put more of himself into his work, to demand more and more of himself—and of his students?

Jana shifted, left leg sliding forward enough to again be in contact with her small son's foot, which had moved away a few inches. *Even in sleep she's aware of needing closeness with the one she loves.*

That observation made Ray suck in his breath sharply. *Even awake, I seldom make an effort to be close to anyone.*

What's wrong with me today? Maybe I'd better just set this plant on the dresser and get out of here. However, he'd told them at the shop that, since he was hand-delivering it, he didn't need a notification-of-sender card stuck in his train engine container.

He put the planter on the bedside table and was getting a business card from his wallet when he heard a sigh and saw Jana open her eyes and look right at him. He was sure he'd made no noise; had she sensed his presence?

She did not seem startled or uneasy at his being there, just smiled sleepily. Something caught in his throat, and he had to swallow hard. She looked so young, and innocent, and sweet, lying there with her arm around her sleeping son, and he had a moment of forcing himself to stay where he was.

What he'd been tempted to do was to push the table aside and take the several steps necessary to put his arms around both of them as they lay there on the bed—something he'd never before have considered doing!

Chapter Two

In her dream she'd just relived Dr. Hawkins saying she had his permission to hold him accountable—then here he was, a few feet away. She smiled lazily, then sobered as she realized where she was, lying in bed with her arm around her son, who'd been so sick.

"Oh...." It was an almost silent interjection as she cautiously straightened her arm, made sure her skirt was covering her thighs, then rolled over to sit on the side of the bed. "I—didn't know you were here," she whispered.

His voice was equally soft. "I just arrived, and I'm glad you were able to sleep. You must have needed it."

She stood up. "I was awake all night."

"Well, I—uh..." He looked almost embarrassed as he picked up the ceramic train engine holding several green plants. "I hoped that maybe your son—your Michael would like this. He's not allergic to just foliage, is he?"

This man is really ill at ease—and I've seen that twice today. I never suspected.... Jana held the gift in both hands. "This is lovely, and I appreciate your considering possible allergies. Several of his worst attacks followed being around Easter lilies, poinsettias and mums—and I suspect carnations, though that was only once."

"Is there anything you can do to control it—shots or anything?"

"It was discussed the last time we were at his pediatrician's—and we're scheduled to see the allergist next week." She glanced toward the calendar on the wall. "Which reminds me to call him today."

They'd moved across the room so they wouldn't be as apt to wake the sleeping child, and she was in the doorway when she saw Gram come around the corner. Jana hurried to meet her and put her arms around the older woman, who was asking, "How is our little sweetheart?"

"Much better! He's still wheezing, but has been sleeping for well over an hour. He hasn't coughed much during that time."

"Good!" But then she cautioned, "Don't be alarmed, though, if he does some when he gets awake."

"I realize he's probably continuing to produce phlegm, and his body will try to loosen it." She briefly wondered about the best way to account for this man being here and decided on making a simple, straightforward introduction. "Gram, this is Dr. Raymond Hawkins. Professor Hawkins, I'd like you to meet Mrs. MaryJean McHenry, one of the most special people I've ever known."

"Ah, yes, the biology professor," Gram said, not looking at all surprised as she stretched out her hand. "I'm pleased to meet you, Dr. Hawkins."

He took the necessary step forward to clasp her hand. "And I'm honored to meet you, Mrs. McHenry."

Gram admired the planter. "Some of our relatives were involved with railroads. There used to be a short line that ran right through Sylvan

Falls, which accounts for our still having a Railroad Street.''

This definitely got his attention, for he asked a number of questions. It was some time later when Gram asked, ''Have you eaten anything, Jana?''

''I was in too much of a hurry to get back here, then didn't want to leave Michael.''

Gram stood there shaking her head. ''Look, dear, you've got to start taking care of yourself, not only for your sake, but his.''

''Granted, but there seem to be exceptions to even the most logical of rules.'' She smiled. ''And, really, that little nap I had with him did me more good than a multicourse dinner.''

''Could be.'' Gram wasn't about to argue, but looked toward Ray. ''Why don't you take Jana down to the cafeteria while I'm here to stay with Michael?''

''Gram!'' She was mortified at Gram's asking him to do that. ''Dr. Hawkins is a busy man. He doesn't have to escort me downstairs!''

But Ray was saying at the same time, ''That's a great suggestion, Mrs. McHenry—especially since I also neglected to eat.''

''But—''

"I don't enjoy always eating alone, Jana, and this is close enough to the evening meal that a sandwich or dish of ice cream later will take care of that."

His smile was almost boyish, and there seemed to be a twinkle in his eye. Jana still didn't feel right about this, but replied, "Wel-l-l, since we both do need to eat, I guess it makes sense to do it now. But if Michael's at all upset about my leaving...."

Gram laughed and raised her hand as though taking an oath. "My dear Jana, I promise to take good care of him."

"I'm sorry. You know more about babies and children than I ever will. It's just that I was so scared last night and this morning."

"Why wouldn't you be? I was, too."

Michael had flopped over on the bed to where Jana had recently been lying, and she wondered if by any chance she'd left some scent there—if it was more than happenstance that made the sleeping child seem to relax. Her arms ached with the almost irrepressible urge to gather her son close, to hold him, but she picked up her small purse and led the way from the room.

They engaged in small talk about college activities. No, she was not involved with any clubs or organizations—except for that noon meeting, which she sometimes attended when staying for an afternoon lab or to work at the library. She'd had no expectation of continuing to talk about that, but did when he asked another question. "It's quite informal. Different people volunteer to read a scripture and share thoughts, and then there's always some discussion and a time of prayer."

"Do *you* volunteer?"

She glanced at him as she led the way into the empty elevator. "Not yet, though I should, for it's been helpful for me."

She wondered if he'd like it, but had no way of knowing, since he changed the subject to something he'd recently read about in an endo-crinology journal as they entered the cafeteria.

She'd expected to have just a bowl of soup and a sandwich, but he talked her into a full meal when he said, "What are the odds that your little one won't want you leaving to eat later?"

"You're right, of course. And by then Gram will be back in Sylvan Falls."

"You're not going to stay here again tonight, are you?"

"I don't expect to, not unless Michael gets worse, which could happen. His attacks usually don't begin until after eleven, most frequently between midnight and two."

"You plan to stay that long?"

He sounded concerned, and she shook her head. "Just until he's asleep—if he's still doing this well. He's ordinarily a good sleeper, so I'm praying we'll *both* rest well tonight."

He nodded, but didn't commit himself to praying for that, as some of her friends might have. For that matter, she had no way of knowing whether he even believed in prayer.

They were sitting across from one another at one of the small square tables when she asked, "Do you have a family?"

He shrugged. "Parents—in Wisconsin, and a sister in Pittsburgh. I don't see as much of them as I'd like."

"Oh?" *I shouldn't have said that—it's none of my business.*

"We're all busy with one thing or another." He seemed to study her before adding, "While working on my degrees, I never had much time for visiting and, though we keep saying we're going to, we've sort of got out of the habit of making the effort.''

"That's too bad.''

"I take it you have strong family ties.''

"No.'' *I shouldn't have started this conversation.* "We don't.''

His brows rose, making horizontal furrows above them. "If I had a grandmother like yours, I'd count myself lucky.''

"I do count myself blessed to have Gram. She's one of the most loving, remarkable women in the world. But she's not....''

"She's not...?''

Why can't I learn to think before speaking? "It's nothing.''

Although one part of her didn't want to say anything more, Ray sat there waiting for her to continue. She finally murmured. "She's not a blood relative, though I wish she were. She took me in when I needed a place to stay.''

Ray's instincts told him not to push this, to let the matter lie, but he could not force himself to eat the food on his fork.

Her gaze had been turned downward when she said that, but lifted, perhaps reluctantly, to meet his. There was such pain there that his hand reached over to cover hers. "It's okay, Jana. You don't owe me explanations."

Her lids flickered, then steadied as she drew in a quick, sharp breath and gave a nod. Neither said anything more for what seemed a long time, and then, after she asked him to pass the salt, he changed the subject to trains.

Ray inquired as to whether she'd been to Steamtown National Park, and when she answered negatively he spent much of the rest of their time together sharing what that was like and talking about specific engines. It didn't matter right then if she was even interested; it was something to say, something to fill that dangerous bog into which they'd almost fallen.

He'd expected to go upstairs to Michael's room with her, but as the elevator doors opened she thanked him for the gift to her son and for the meal he'd insisted on paying for even though she had stated she'd prefer doing that herself.

Well, I've now blown it twice today as far as she's concerned! That was not a happy thought as the door closed behind her and he turned to cross the lobby alone. The first time had been because of superciliousness, but perhaps his inquisitiveness might be just as bad, or worse.

He considered following her, and even reached to push the elevator's up button, but stopped in time. Gram was undoubtedly still there, her little boy might be awake—and what could he say or do to make things better, anyway? *I guess the only thing is to hope for the best in class tomorrow. But if her friends are with her when she leaves, like today, it would only embarrass her if I apologize for making such a fool of myself this second time.*

Gram was holding Michael on her lap, reading one of the books she'd brought. He looked over and started talking even while removing his thumb from his mouth. "Gram's reading *Mr. Hoppity's Happiest Harvest,* my extra-fav'rite special book."

Jana ran her fingers across the top of his head, relishing the caress of the fine, golden-brown hair slipping between them. "That's one of my favorites, too."

Squirming around, he pointed toward the straight chair near them. "Gram can read to you, too, Mama."

"I'd like that, but there are things I should read for my classes. If that's all right with you, Gram."

"I'm staying for another hour or so." Gram smiled encouragement. "You do your thing, dear, and Michael and I will do ours, 'cause we just *love* to read books."

He leaned against her shoulder and, just before his thumb returned to his mouth, agreed, "Yep, me and Gram just love reading books."

Jana smiled at the two people she loved most in the world and carried her books and notebook to the plastic chair by the window. *Thanks, God, for Michael's being so much better, and thanks for Gram, with all her goodness and love. And please help me use this next hour or so efficiently, because I don't know how much more time I'll have to study.*

One of the many good things about living at Gram's was that she'd been forced to compartmentalize. There were people around all the time, and so many activities—especially with the children!—that she'd never have survived these college years had she not been able to fix her attention on just one or two things at a time, while yet not being blind to her surroundings.

She finished the reading assignments and was

working on problems for statistics when Gram got to her feet and said she'd have to leave. Michael wasn't happy about that, clinging to her and begging her to stay. It was hard for Jana not to get involved, but she was glad she'd refrained when Gram set the crying child on his bed and took both of his little hands in hers. "Michael, dear, you know I always tell you the truth, don't you?"

"Uh-huh. But...."

"And I've already told you that either you will come home to be with me tomorrow, or I will come here and be with you, right?"

"Uh-huh, but..." He tried again.

"But right now, I am needed at home."

Tears ran down his cheeks, but he nodded.

After Gram left, Jana read several more books to him then, at the beginning of the hour, checked through various TV channels until she found one suitable for her son to watch as she worked on assignments.

He pushed the evening meal away when an aide brought it, but his program was so filled with fast action that Jana was able to spoon food into his mouth without his realizing it.

She never did this at home—didn't have to; he was an excellent eater, and nobody watched TV at mealtime. So much conversation took place around Gram's big kitchen table that there wouldn't be time to stare at a television screen.

They took another walk past the elevators and to the end of the long hallway. At first she tried to go slowly, not wanting increased activity to give Michael a setback, but that didn't last long; even when several of the staff greeted him by name, he was too busy investigating gurneys, potted plants, wheelchairs and other things to remain long with anyone.

He slowed down some as they neared his room again, but he didn't complain about being put back in his bed since she lay down beside him. This, too, she usually didn't do, but Jana wanted to make things as easy as possible for him in this strange place. She was just starting another book when Gram's granddaughter, Karlyn, came to visit.

Michael was yawning by the time Karlyn left. Jana explained that she'd be going home later so he could sleep better in his bed but she'd be back in the morning—probably before they brought breakfast. In the meantime, she took him to the bathroom after he drank the orange juice and ate several graham crackers brought to him by an aide, then said she'd lie beside him to read some more.

She finally stated, with a deliberately obvious yawn, that she was very tired—but did have to struggle to keep from dropping off before he did!

It was almost too dark to see the multicolored flowers of bulbs and trees and golden forsythia as Jana drove home through the late April evening. She of course recognized the cars parked by the curb in front of Gram's house, so she knew AnnaMae and Kate had come to pick up their children.

Barb had offered to cover for Jana in giving childcare this afternoon, and it seemed almost incomprehensible that, at first, the two of them had not got along well. They were as close as sisters now, probably closer than many siblings—but then they'd been two lonely, scared, pregnant sixteen-year-olds whom Gram had taken into her home, along with the three slightly older girls in the same situation, Kate, AnnaMae and Ricki.

Barb came onto the veranda as Jana started up the walk to Gram's huge old Victorian house. "How's our little sweetheart?"

"Although he continues to cough and wheeze some, he seems good, and everyone thinks he's okay. If he gets through tonight without an attack, perhaps he'll come home tomorrow." She climbed the front steps. "What about things here?"

"Mary has a runny nose, but seems to feel all right. I don't think she's coming down with a cold. And the other kids are fine."

Jana nodded toward the cars out front. "I see AnnaMae and Kate have come for their little ones."

"And Ricki was covering this evening, so they'll all soon be gone."

They entered the large front hall and were greeted by the three children. Jana laid her purse on the floor as she got down on her knees to hug them. "I missed you guys," she said, kissing each of them.

Their mothers came from the kitchen to get the latest update on Michael before leaving for the night—and suddenly it seemed very quiet with just the three adults. Gram looked around. "It's almost lonely with no children in the house."

Barb nodded. "It seems eons ago when it was just you, Gram and us five teens."

"And much longer when I was living alone here." She sighed. "Thank goodness I didn't fully realize what I was missing."

Jana remembered how frightened she'd been

before coming here as one of the five pregnant teens Gram had taken under her wing. At that time, it had been considered a safe haven where they could stay until their babies were born— after which each infant would go to adoptive parents.

But she didn't want to think about that now. "To hear your family, especially your granddaughter, Andi, tell it, you kept just as busy then!"

"I enjoyed everything I was doing, but not nearly as much as having you and the other girls and the little ones around."

Jana had no doubt that was true, and her arm slid around the older woman's trim waist. "I got to thinking last night that what we call you is also your title, your profession. You *are* Gram to half the people in Sylvan Falls—but especially to us!"

"What a sweet thing to say. I don't deserve it, but I'll treasure it anyway." She beamed at Jana, smiled at Barb and headed for the kitchen. "Come get a piece of apple pie, then you get to bed, Jana. I'm sure you need your rest!"

"Sounds like two wonderful ideas." She followed Gram and Barb and thoroughly enjoyed the dessert. Getting up from the table a little later,

Jana remembered to tell them, "I'm setting my alarm for the last possible moment—so don't think I've overslept."

But her final thoughts before falling asleep were about Dr. Ray Hawkins bringing the plants to the hospital for her son, and of his being so kind, so nice as they ate together.

Having planned to be in the classroom earlier than usual, Ray considered not answering the phone as he was leaving his office. But he did, and the message was important; however, he still begrudged the time.

All the students were seated before he arrived, but he had no difficulty spotting Jana, halfway back in the middle row. Laying down his books, he asked, even while walking around the front table, "I trust your son is better this morning, Ms. Jenson?"

She looked startled, and he wondered if that was because, although always willing to answer anything or talk about science, he almost always stuck to lesson material. He hoped she'd recognized this as something of a public apology on his part when she answered, "Yes, thank you. Michael's improved so much that we hope he'll be discharged today."

"Good!" Ray commented, then proceeded to begin the day's lesson.

After the class was over, Todd and Linda walked out with Jana again. Ray couldn't control the spontaneous smile that came to his face as she passed his table—and was inordinately pleased that her responding one seemed genuine. *But even with that beautiful smile of hers, I'm afraid she won't forget yesterday. It's not appropriate for me to ask her to have lunch with me— especially in front of her friends. Anyway, I shouldn't even consider becoming friends with a young woman who's the mother of a small child!*

Is there a husband somewhere? Has she ever had one? I know that's not supposed to matter anymore, but it does to me. And I don't know a thing about small children and shouldn't even be thinking of that child—or his mother. Which, as the day went on, he found to be a difficult resolution to keep.

"Are you staying for the meeting today, Jana?" Todd asked, walking over to Richards Hall with her.

"I hadn't thought that far ahead."

"It's not much more than an hour from now."

"I know. Somehow Michael's illness seems to

have driven away other thoughts—not that God isn't even more important, but...."

"I wasn't being judgmental. It's just that I was hoping you'd be there today."

"*Especially* today?"

"Well, yes." His grin was a bit lopsided. "I'm the one leading devotions."

She laid a hand on his arm. "In that case, I'll surely come. This will be my first time to hear you do that."

"I've never volunteered before and I'll admit to being sort of scared—at least nervous."

"I would be, too, yet we both know there's no one there to critique you. Everyone's encouraging—supportive."

"*You* haven't volunteered, either."

"And I probably won't. Public speaking doesn't seem to be one of my gifts."

"I felt that way, too, then got to thinking I shouldn't just keep receiving. It was time for giving, too."

"Then it's right for you," she agreed. "But thus far I haven't been convinced of that for me."

She thought for a moment that he was about to argue, but they were nearing her classroom, so she gave him a smile and went inside. *I know he has other friends there, but it must mean something to him for me to be supportive, too.*

The professor gave a pop quiz at the beginning of class, making Jana especially grateful for having disciplined herself to do that assignment.

Class ran a bit late, so by the time she got to the lounge in Sanderson Dorm where the noon meeting was held the circle of seats was nearly full. These get-togethers were always informal. Today, like most others, the two choruses they sang were unaccompanied, yet harmonized.

Jana had been in the junior high and senior high choruses back home and had been chosen to sing solos several times—but she mustn't think about such enjoyable things now. That was a different place and a different time; she and her parents had been on reasonably good terms then.

Before she got pregnant. Before she had to leave home. Before her comfortable world had fallen apart.

Todd asked one of the freshmen to read a chosen scripture, and a senior led in prayer. He then went directly into his fifteen-minute meditation on reaching out to others, to being a friend under all situations. He seemed to glance toward Jana more than she wished, but she considered the talk good, especially for a first one. She commended him on this before hurrying home.

Gram had brought Michael home from the hospital in mid-morning, and he was already taking his afternoon nap by the time Jana got there. Although Gram reported that he seemed to be doing all right, Jana tiptoed in to gently place her hand against his forehead and on his chest to verify that his temperature and breathing were normal.

Downstairs, she took over her shift as babysitter. In addition to the four children who were usually here, Gram's great-granddaughter, Katherine, had been brought by her father, Keith.

Ricki had left for her part-time job after explaining that her daughter, Debbie, seemed more fussy than usual. "She's not running an elevated temp or anything, and Gram and I don't think she's coming down with anything. She insisted she wasn't sleepy, but you know what an agreeable doll she usually is. I put her to bed anyway and hope for your sake, as well as hers, that she's in a better mood when she gets up."

Gram was spending time at the library with her literacy volunteer work. She'd not done this for the last several years, but with everyone pulling together so well, she'd decided to get back to the work she so loved.

Jana opened her books on the kitchen table, realizing chances were good that at least one of the five children would soon be waking. Then she went upstairs to the room she shared with her son, opened the desk drawer as silently as possible and removed several boxes to take downstairs.

She didn't find what she wanted in the assortment of greetings, but among her note cards was a black-and-white sketch of a steam engine pulling a coal car and an assortment of others, including passenger, box, container, flatbed and animal—and there was also, of course, a caboose.

A smile was on her face while writing the thank-you note to Ray, and she'd still heard no sounds from upstairs by the time the envelope was sealed, stamped and carried to the front porch. Today's mail had not yet been delivered, so Jana clipped her envelope to the wall-mounted mailbox for pickup.

She disciplined herself to write a brief letter to her parents, as she'd promised herself to do each week, even though she had heard nothing from them for all these years. She always had her return address on the envelope, and none had been returned so, still hoping they were being read, she continued to write, each missive accompanied by a prayer for reconciliation.

Both Mother and Dad had told her that if she didn't care enough for them to do as they commanded, to have that abortion, they would no longer consider her to be their daughter. However, she'd continued to inform them of most things, especially of Michael's birth, of her graduation from high school and of being almost finished with her third year of college.

She'd sent photocopies of report cards, but those consistently above 3.5 grade point averages got no more acknowledgment than had the announcement of the birth of their only grandchild. Nevertheless, she wrote a few lines about Michael's recent hospitalization and his being home again.

Her studying wasn't completed, but at least she'd made a good start on the second subject before going upstairs to bring down the first two children. Everything was left on the table in case she might have a few more minutes this afternoon, although that was unlikely. Whatever was undone by then would be tackled again after the little girls went home and Michael was put to bed for the night—if she could stay awake and alert enough to do so.

Chapter Three

Ray had gone over his notes for the next class and was treating himself to a break—reading the lead article in the current *Trains* magazine. Lost in the account of an early logging railroad, he barely looked up when the student serving as to-day's deliverer of faculty mail tapped on his nearly closed door. "You got lots of stuff this morning, Professor."

"Thanks." He reached for the rubber-banded bundle and started to set it on the corner of the desk when he noticed the hand-addressed square envelope with no return address.

He slit it open with the slender ivory knife given to him by his grandfather years before and smiled when he pulled out the enclosed card. He guessed from whom it came before unfolding it. Who else would choose one with that fanciful picture of a train? The message was relatively informal:

Dear Dr. Hawkins,
Michael and I would like to thank you again for your thoughtfulness in choosing and delivering the delightful train-engine container and plants. He has loved trains ever since I first read to him the book *Terry Tooter,* and he has several picture books featuring them.

I also appreciate your giving so generously of your time and concern in seeing to it that I ate lunch—my dinner, actually.

My son is home again now and seems to be doing well.

And I want to apologize for my almost-yawn in class. Believe me, I have never been bored there; you are an excellent teacher, and I'm grateful for the opportunity of being one of your students.

Sincerely,
Jana Jenson

He smiled and read the card twice before sliding it back into its envelope and opening the top center drawer of his desk. Instead of placing it there, however, he tucked it into his shirt pocket, glanced at the wall clock and started for his classroom. Jana arrived perhaps a minute later with her friend Linda Patterson; although they both greeted him with a good morning, he was annoyed at his response coming out so stupidly imitative!

By the middle of the period he knew he must make an opportunity to speak with her. After all, this was Friday; tonight was his monthly train meeting.

Jana had not exaggerated in writing that she liked his teaching; Dr. Hawkins was enthusiastic about his subject, and she always made notes of material he shared with them from current journals. He'd horrified many when his first test included questions based on this information as well as what was in textbooks, but she'd answered everything correctly; she, too, was fascinated by human embryology.

The fifty minutes passed almost too quickly, and she started forward by herself as Todd and

Linda were discussing something with another student. As she passed the front table, Dr. Hawkins asked how Michael was this morning. She paused long enough to say that he seemed almost as good as normal. "Little ones bounce back much faster than a parent does."

"Although they feel rotten, I guess maybe they don't worry about it like adults."

"That does make a huge difference," she agreed. "And there's no way to keep him from running and playing hard with the other children—which may be good. As shook-up as I was, I'd undoubtedly be overprotective."

The other three students had left the classroom but, though out of sight in the hallway, they were talking and laughing nearby. Suddenly, Dr. Hawkins cleared his throat and said, "Look, Jana, our railroad meeting's tonight. It starts at six with a catered buffet, then there's a program with slides concerning one of this region's short line railroads. Perhaps it would be good for you to get away from things for a bit, and I think you'd enjoy it, and the people...."

He'd spoken quietly but more rapidly than usual, and he was obviously ill at ease, which made her hesitate. The situation became more awkward when he added, "I'd like to take you with me."

I can hardly believe this. "I may be needed at home."

"Could you call and see if your grandmother or someone could take care of things?" A strained look crossed his face as he amended, "Take care of your son?"

Her books had been held tight against her chest, and she consciously tried to relax a little, pleased to be asked but cautious. "I haven't dated for a very long time, Dr. Hawkins, and...."

"You needn't think of this as a date, maybe just—you know, having a change of pace, hearing and seeing things unconnected with sickness or classes or anything."

I'd have laughed had anyone suggested that this man would ask me out—and that I'd be tempted to go! But I would enjoy doing something different, and I do like what I know of him.

He pulled back the hand that had seemed to start reaching toward her and suggested, "You can phone from my office."

Two of the students in the hallway had moved on, but Todd was there and took a step in their direction. He had perhaps noted the hand almost touching her arm, so she spoke before he could. "I'm going to use the professor's phone again, Todd, to check on Michael."

His questioning look changed to concern. "Is he worse?"

"He seemed good this morning, but I'll feel better after making sure."

"I'll wait for you."

"Thanks, but you have another class, too. There's no point in both of us being late." He did leave, but she saw him glance back before going out of sight.

Jana probably wouldn't have noticed her drawn-out sigh had she not seen the professor's smile—and found herself smiling back. She made her call, but the phone wasn't picked up until the sixth ring. "Hello?"

"Kate? I wasn't sure you'd be home yet."

"Just came in the door." She sounded breathless. "I had to stop for gas."

"I was wondering how Michael's doing."

"He and Mary are playing with blocks here on the kitchen floor, so I'm fairly sure he's okay. I'll check with Gram."

"Could I talk to her for a minute?"

"Sure, hold on."

And then she heard Gram's cheerfully reassuring voice. "Michael's doing great, Jana."

"Not even wheezing?"

"Oh, a little—like before you left this morning—and there's an occasional cough. Nothing more than that."

"Wonderful! I thought he'd be all right, but I had to make sure."

Gram chuckled. "Good mothers are like that."

Gram's approval brought a smile to her lips, but then Jana glanced toward Ray, standing by the window, looking outside, obviously trying to give her the impression of privacy as she made her request. "Professor Hawkins asked if I'd like to go with him to a train meeting this evening— a buffet supper and slide program. I was wondering whether—"

"Of course, dear," Gram said without waiting for further explanation. "I don't have a thing planned for the rest of the day, so Michael and I can have fun spending it together."

"You're sure? I don't have to go—"

"But you'd like to?"

"Well, yes. I would."

"Then by all means do so, Jana. It's about

time you have a life beyond this house, the
church and college.''

Gram's words had sounded like good advice
when said this morning, but flocks of butterflies
were fluttering in Jana's stomach by five o'clock.
Dr. Hawkins had said she could wear anything,
for this group was very informal. She'd finally
decided on a flowered cotton skirt and sleeveless
blouse, then changed that for a short-sleeved one.
And, just before he was to arrive, she decided on
jeans instead of the skirt.

He was in the hallway when she ran down the
wide, spindle-banistered stairs. ''Hi.''

He'd been greeted by Gram, who took a step
backward so he could move toward Jana. ''You
look lovely, as always.''

''Thanks.'' That surprised her a little—and she
still wasn't sure about her attire. ''Are jeans and
a blouse suitable for tonight?''

''You'll fit right in,'' he assured her. ''A few
women wear skirts or dresses, but most are in
jeans or shorts. Something casual.''

Michael had come in and was leaning against
Jana's leg, so she reached down to run her hand
along his shoulder and arm. ''Michael, this is Dr.

Hawkins, the nice man who brought you the train filled with plants.''

The corners of Michael's lips turned up just a little, though he didn't remove his thumb from his mouth even when the professor said, ''I hope you're feeling better.''

The child only nodded, but Jana didn't insist on his politely expressing gratitude; his mother's leaving with a man was not a usual occurrence, and she could only hope he wouldn't make a fuss. Her voice was light as she said, ''Michael, dear, I'm going with Dr. Hawkins to a special meeting, so you and Gram will get to eat together all by yourself this time.''

He wasn't ready for that. He reached for her hand and held it tight. ''Don't go, Mama! Eat with us.''

It was Gram who took care of this by taking his other hand. ''Let's go to the kitchen, sweetheart. Maybe you can help me find some of that ham left over from dinner last night, and some cheese. And you can decide whether to have peas or baby carrots for our vegetable.''

He looked less than enthusiastic about any of this until she added, ''And there are red grapes for dessert, after we finish the other things.''

He released his mother's hand and led the way to the kitchen. "I know where the ham is, Gram—in the frigrator's bottom drawer!"

Gram followed him, her words soft-spoken. "Don't worry about things here. You two just have a good time!"

Ray saw the uncertainty in Jana's dark blue eyes when her gaze followed her little boy as he ran into the kitchen. *She doesn't leave Michael much except for school.* Ray couldn't have told how he knew, but he was sure that was true. "Shall we go?" he asked briskly. "They normally begin serving right on time."

She looked at him with an almost self-deprecating smile and slid her hand through his slightly bent arm. "Yes, I—guess it's time."

She means something different from time as of right now. Perhaps it's time for a change, but I haven't a clue as to whether that's in regard to me or tonight's program or dating. As they walked out the door, across the porch and to his car, he spoke of the beautiful weather and the spring flowers, and she responded with comments more brief than his.

The drive took about a half hour, and by then

he'd asked not only about her other classes but her post-graduation plans. "I'm not sure," she confessed, "and that's awful when I'm almost through my third year."

He deliberately kept from commenting or even looking at her, for he sensed that the wrong response might make her withdraw. There was a brief silence before she said, "I started out working toward a degree in psychology, with an emphasis on children, then I switched to early childhood education."

This pause was so long that he turned to look at her. At first he thought she was fine, sitting there looking out the windshield, hands clasped in her lap, but then it registered that those slender hands were tightly gripping one another. "You no longer care much for either of those majors?"

She looked startled, then gave a little laugh. "Much of what I'm taught is excellent, and I'm at the top of the class gradewise, but in all good conscience I couldn't go along with some of it, should my job demand that."

"So where does that leave you?" he asked.

She raised her shoulders in a somewhat embarrassed shrug. "I tell myself I must soon decide that."

"So what are your top options as of now?"

"Well, I'm seriously considering social work involving young mothers and their children—yet the fact that I'll be the sole breadwinner makes me wonder if the relatively low salary I'd probably earn is fair to Michael."

She shifted position on the seat, looking out the passenger window, perhaps hoping he'd change the topic, but he asked, "Do you know anyone professionally involved in that field?"

"I wish I did. The thing is, I do know Gram, whose stubborn faith in individuals and her love for them has accomplished the almost impossible in many lives. I'm not finding enough of that in the texts or in my teachers."

He wondered how Jana was being supported now; was it Gram's largess? But he supposed that, being a single mother, she could be receiving subsidies or other help from government programs. Or, if she was separated or divorced, she might at least be getting child support. He'd not ask such a prying question; it was none of his business, and she was probably the kind of person who'd be embarrassed about accepting any help.

"It's hard for many of us to know what we

want to be when we grow up," he admitted, deliberately wording that in a less-than-serious fashion.

"Don't tell me that you, a full professor, are considering a change."

Why did I say that? I haven't mentioned it to anyone! However, he continued, "There are times in many lives when the grass doesn't look as green on our side of the fence as we'd expected."

She didn't drop it there, and he had no right not to answer her next question after prying into her business. "Were I starting over, I'd seriously consider becoming a physician."

"Really?" Her face was alight with what appeared to be wonder. "What kind of doctor would you like to be?"

"I grew up in a relatively small Wisconsin town, and the person I most admired there was Dr. Philip Posten, an elderly general practitioner who seemed to know everything.

"He not only brought children into the world, but was there to support their great-grandparents on the way out of it. He always seemed to be available—and was one of the most loving, most concerned people in my universe."

"So you dream of being like him." It was a statement. "It sounds like you have a wonderful model, as Gram is mine," Jana said.

It was time to pull off the main highway, which made him realize he'd better straighten out something immediately. "I'd like to ask a favor, Jana."

She nodded, and he stated, "That about my considering a change of direction—possibly becoming an M.D.—I'd appreciate your not mentioning that to anyone."

"Of course not. It's no one's business."

"I haven't discussed this with anyone before."

"Not anyone?"

She looked puzzled, and he was, himself, wondering why he'd told her this. "Not anyone."

Eager to change the subject and to be where they were heading, he said, "We're almost there, Jana. Through this underpass, then here we make a left. See? There's our station house along the track."

Jana had neglected to ask where the station was located and realized she'd many times passed it on the main highway not much over a quarter-mile from here and never noticed the large, one-story building.

She saw the railroad cars he'd mentioned, several in fairly good condition, others rusty and dirty. She paid close attention as Ray told of the terrible condition in which this neatly restored brick station had been until fifteen years ago, and how the members worked so hard to fix it.

He parked among the twenty or so cars, trucks and motorcycles. She didn't wait for him to come around to assist her from his vehicle, but suddenly felt out of place. She knew nobody except the professor and knew little about trains or restoration.

Just as Ray reached Jana's side, a middle-aged man who'd pulled in right behind them called, "Wait up, Ray! I've got something to show you."

The man and his wife were introduced as Sam and Penny Rafferty. Mr. Rafferty was excited about a recently acquired picture postcard of this very station, postmarked seventy-two years earlier. "Just look at this, Ray. We got the colors exactly right when we painted her!"

"We did." Ray then explained to Jana, "There were faded, flaking remains of the cream and green and browns of the trim, and we also knew what some of the area stations looked like, but no one had proof of the shades here.''

Jana tried to be enthusiastic but was relieved when Mrs. Rafferty nudged her arm and, eyes sparkling, stated, ''I swear Sam was more excited at finding that at an Allentown flea market than if he'd come upon the Hope diamond!''

That made Jana feel more comfortable; apparently not everyone needed to be gung ho about trains and stations. She was introduced to person after person, to couples and to groups, all apparently knowing Ray well and liking him—and more than ready to welcome and get to know her.

They all called him Ray, but Jana felt she shouldn't, seeing that he was her college professor. Yet, having come with him and thus knowing that people probably assumed they were dating, she could hardly address him as doctor, either. Therefore she carefully refrained from calling him anything—which sometimes seemed awkward.

The meal had been laid out on tables arranged in a U-shape in the first of the three elongated building's rooms. This would have been the waiting room, as there was a ticket window chest-high in the middle of the wall separating it from the narrower office.

Several steps led up to a much larger area, which had to be where freight and baggage were kept until ready to be loaded or picked up. As they entered the first room, Ray had pointed out to her the upward-sloping ramp leading to the platform just outside the huge door, built at the exact height of and right next to where boxcars, cattle cars or other rolling stock were on the siding.

Chairs had been carried outside to form informal groups, and Jana enjoyed those in their circle—the Raffertys, Paul and Judy Merchant, who were probably in their mid-seventies, and Alta Jones, a recent widow who'd come with the Merchants.

In class, Ray of course carried the ball as to speaking, but here she was impressed by his being an equally good listener. They'd gone inside for their pie and ice cream and were returning with the desserts when Mrs. Jones said to Jana, "My late husband, Ben, and I lived in Sylvan Falls for the twelve years he was principal of the high school. We made some good friends there."

One of those she mentioned was Gin Redding,

and when Jana told her this woman was Gram's very good friend and next-door neighbor, the widow was delighted. "And to think you live with MaryJean McHenry! Isn't she wonderful?"

"The finest woman I've ever had the privilege of knowing."

"She's the one who got me started with my literacy work!" Mrs. Jones told her friends before asking, "I assume she's still doing that, right?"

"Yes, she is." It wasn't necessary to say that she'd stopped her volunteer work for several years when she'd taken Jana and four other pregnant girls into her home.

"I wonder how many people she's helped that way. It's got to be hundreds." Mrs. Jones's admiration was obvious. "And she used to be active in the Volunteer Firemen's Auxiliary. Did she continue that after her husband was killed in that awful fire?"

"Oh, yes, she still makes all the sauce for those hundreds of chicken quarters they barbecue during carnival week, and bakes pies and does many other things. But—" Jana paused and laughed "—Gram claims she's slowing down."

Jana saw Ray smile, but she felt anything but

relaxed when Mrs. Jones asked, "How did you happen to go live with her?"

Jana took time to set her glass of iced tea on her tray before looking at the older woman. "I guess I'm just lucky, Mrs. Jones."

It had been something to say, and she couldn't retract those words, even though she was positive luck had nothing to do with it.

Ray thought he detected a tenseness in Jana, even though she sounded normal. When he mentioned something about the postcard they'd seen, he was sure he saw Jana smile and look at him in relief. She leaned toward him, saying she'd like to look more closely at the sign over the office door as shown on the picture, and then the others became involved in that discussion.

It wasn't long before the announcement was made that their meeting would soon begin inside. As Jana and Mrs. Rafferty gathered what would be thrown into the garbage, Mrs. Jones took the trays to the waiting room and the men folded the chairs preparatory to carrying them up the ramp.

The women went outside to follow them through the opening made by pushing back the mammoth square door on its extended overhead track and Mrs. Rafferty commended, "Well done, boys—getting us seats right up here in the second row."

Ray grinned. "That's what we like, appreciation." He reached for Jana's arm as she stood at the end of the row. "Are you okay with sitting here?"

"I'd like that."

It was said so softly he was sure the others didn't hear, and he thought her expression was—what? Relief? Was she conscious of holding his hand tightly as he took the seat between her and the others with whom they'd eaten?

He wished she'd leave it there but had to release his grip as she slid her hand from his.

New arrivals stopped to talk with him and the others and undoubtedly to be introduced to his lovely young guest. When nobody else was speaking to them, Jana asked about artifacts on shelves, in showcases and hanging on the walls—but he hadn't covered even all those nearest to them when the president began the brief meeting.

And then it was time for the showing of slides and telling the history of a rail line in northern Pennsylvania, which had been invaluable while the region was part of the greatest lumber area of the world, but did not survive once that era was over.

Jana seemed fascinated by everything, so much so that her questions and his answers filled the too-short trip back to Sylvan Falls. Before he knew it he was walking her to her front door, and she was thanking him for a wonderful evening— and going inside.

Leaving him there.

I've just blown another opportunity! He'd been waiting for an especially good time to ask if he could take her to the station on Sunday; they could go through the cars, perhaps first a couple of the semi-restored ones, then some in the deplorable condition in which the club had acquired them.

She would in that way get a better idea how involved he and many of the others were. And he was fairly sure she'd enjoy climbing into the engine, and he could explain how things worked.

He'd even decided that if she seemed hesitant about going with him—especially so soon after tonight—he'd suggest that they take Michael with them. As devoted to her son as she appeared to be, Ray figured she might agree to that.

The evening had flown by with her beside him,

and he could only hope they'd have many more good times together. He realized it wasn't just that she was pretty and smart, but he respected and admired her—and hoped she'd go out with him again. Soon!

Chapter Four

❧

Gram's door was open and the light on, so Jana stopped before going to her room. "Getting caught up with your reading?" she asked, seeing the older woman propped up with pillows against the headboard.

Gram laughed. "I do go to the library to help, but can never resist looking at each new book that comes in. I have yet to return home without at least one."

"That's something I'm looking forward to come summer. With all the schoolwork and the kids, I find almost no time to read for pleasure."

"I know." Gram patted the bedside nearest the door as she shifted closer to the center of the big bed she'd slept in alone all these years since her husband was killed. "I recall many times during my younger days when I felt quite deprived as to books."

Jana accepted the invitation to sit down and said, "To be perfectly honest, though, I wouldn't change much if I could. I love every one of these little ones and, though I do grouse about assignments or having to write papers, I'm enjoying— and am so very grateful for college!"

"And the teachers?"

"If you're inquiring as to the one I was with tonight—" she paused and laughed "—yes, I enjoyed being with Dr. Hawkins."

"He seems nice."

"Everyone in his railroad club appears to like him, and I appreciate getting to know that he has a sense of humor and that he's knowledgeable about trains and history and lots of other things besides embryos and hormones and assorted biological facts and phenomena."

"Did he ask you out again?"

She shook her head. "No, but I wouldn't be surprised if he does. At this point, he has no idea about my situation except that I'm Michael's mother and that I live with you. And, as you know, I've done almost no dating since I came here, so I didn't give him opportunity to say or do much once we got to the porch. I just told him what a pleasant evening I had, thanked him for that and came inside.''

''Did he seem…surprised?''

She hadn't thought of it like that. ''I believe he'd have liked the evening to last longer but didn't push the matter—or insist on a hug or kiss or anything.'' Jana stood up and covered a yawn with her hand before adding, as she left the room, ''Who knows? We'll see how things go in class tomorrow.''

All in all, she was pleased. It had been a new and different experience, and whether or not he asked her out again, she'd enjoyed being with him and his friends. It was totally different from her last date, over a year earlier. John Billingsley had known she was an unmarried mother; perhaps that's what led him to expect that her morals were such that he assumed the dinner he took her to entitled him to sexual favors.

She shuddered with revulsion at recalling his attempts to seduce her. *Will I ever be able to really trust a man, given my previous relationship with my son's father?* But she wasn't going to think of that anymore, she decided as she crossed the large hallway and entered the room she shared with her marvelous little boy lying there spread-eagled on his twin bed.

She changed into her nightgown and went to the bathroom before kissing the back of Michael's hand, lying near the edge of his bed, and then went to her own bed.

I don't know if this could be considered a "date," but I enjoyed this time with Dr. Hawkins—Ray—and his friends so very much....

By that next morning Ray had to admit that getting to his classroom early again was more than professionalism, but even while speaking to those first few arrivals he was aware of listening for a certain lilting voice or soft laugh.

However, Jana got there right on time and again was accompanied by Todd Livingston. It was possible they'd met on the way to class, but he couldn't help wondering if there was something going on between those two. Ray somehow thought Jana wouldn't have gone to the train meeting last night if she was seriously interested in another man, but what did he know?

She smiled and said, "Good morning, Doctor,'' which he acknowledged by repeating her first two words. She walked on, of course, and again took a seat about halfway back in the middle row.

It was one minute past the hour, according to the wall clock, and time for the professor persona to be given full rein. ''Before we officially begin today's lesson, I'd like to share an article I came across in one of my journals last night....''

So he didn't go home and right to sleep. And his gaze did remain on mine as he said good morning. And he was smiling, but I'm not at all sure that meant anything personal. And why should it?

But one part of her mind suggested there was just as good a reason to ask, *Why shouldn't it?* and she preferred that possibility.

She straightened in her seat, disciplining herself to take notes on the information being given as well as on the rest of his well-prepared and interesting lecture. Afterward, he was speaking with two students who often stayed to talk after class, and she thought he wasn't aware of her leaving, for she was almost to the door before she heard his voice. ''Ms. Jenson, I wanted to ask how your son is today.''

"He had a very good night, Dr. Hawkins." She felt the smile forming on her face as she turned and took a step in his direction, as he'd done in hers.

But the two students came with him and started asking questions and talking until Jana was forced to leave for her next class. Ray gave her a somewhat lopsided smile and commented, "Have a good day, Jana."

He'd said that softly, gently—and his smile seemed to mean something more than the spoken words. *Don't do this to yourself. Don't set yourself up for pain or loss. You were so gullible four years ago, but you're a grown woman now, a woman with a wonderful child and friends and opportunities.*

But let's face it—although he seemed good with Michael, what makes you think he could ever accept your past—your having an out-of-wedlock child?

She went home after her next class. Having no afternoon ones that day, she could take over for Barb, who was watching the children, as well as eat with her extended family. She didn't fret much about Michael's still not being very hungry and was grateful for his willingness to be put to bed for his nap earlier than usual. Although Michael usually bounced right back, these really bad attacks took a lot out of him.

And of her!

Barb had been able to do a little more studying during the morning, but left as soon as lunch was over. There were many things at school she needed to help take care of, for tonight was the big open house, and the students in the Food Services program at the technical institute had been responsible for planning and preparing the menu, making all purchases and doing all of the actual food preparation and decorating.

Barb finished her intensive two-year course at the institute last year, and had received her associate degree. However, she'd decided to stay on for the additional two years of the newly expanded course leading to a baccalaureate.

With her excellent marks and references, she'd received several good offers from high-class restaurants. As it turned out, however, she'd politely refused all offers, explaining her recent decision to continue her education and asking that she be remembered following the next two years. As none of these offers had been from within their general area, however, Jana hoped with Barb, and expected, that she'd next year receive an even better offer, perhaps within driving distance of Sylvan Falls.

Gram went to the library to meet with one of her literacy students, and Jana used the children's nap time to sweep and dust, since it was her turn to take care of these tasks.

She did not enter any of the bedrooms to clean, not wanting to chance waking the little ones. But, finishing the other dusting, Jana went to the room she shared with Michael, who was sound asleep.

She'd not caught up yet with her sleep and had no expectation of doing that now as she stretched out on top of her bedspread. Startled by the phone's ringing, she realized when glancing at the clock as she hurried to the hall phone that she'd slept for at least a half hour.

"Hello, Jana." It was Ray! "Is this a convenient time to talk for a minute or two?"

"It's fine. The children are asleep and…"

"You—you have more than the one child, your Michael?"

"Only Michael. But three children of dear friends are here much of the time, as well as Gram's great-granddaughter. All the children are approximately the same age."

"Wow! What a busy place you must have!"

"To put it mildly!" she agreed. "But everyone pulls together around college and work schedules."

"I'm impressed!"

"Actually, Gram's the catalyst who makes it happen."

"I think I'd like getting to know her better."

"I assure you it would be well worth your while." *I almost said, I hope you will some day!*

There seemed to be a slight pause before Ray said, "Do you suppose that could be arranged on Sunday afternoon when—if I come to pick up you and Michael? I'd like to take both of you down to the station again, if you think you'd like to go inside the cars and up into the engine— stuff like that."

She didn't need to even think about that! "He'd love to see them, and so would I. What time did you have in mind?"

"Would one or one-fifteen work for you? Or would that interfere with his afternoon nap?"

How thoughtful of him! "He might get a short one on the way. I didn't notice how long it took to drive there."

"About a half hour—maybe a bit longer."

"Well, even a few minutes will tide him over. And is it okay for me to wear jeans?"

"The ideal clothes for the occasion—that's what I'm wearing, too. Things are far from spotless there!"

She laughed. "I've just finished sweeping and dusting here, and was again reminded about things getting dirty all too soon!"

"That's true even in my office at school and my bachelor apartment."

When she hung up the phone a minute or so later, she was not at all surprised that the tall mirror in the hallway showed a radiant smile on her face.

Is it possible she'll recognize my deliberately mentioning my bachelor apartment? I hope so, for I don't want her thinking I might be married. He had no way of knowing, however, nor much more opportunity to add anything, since she'd said she must do some studying before the children awoke.

But she had taken time to say that she and Michael would look forward to seeing the trains on Sunday afternoon.

Well! He'd be having the opportunity of seeing her again day after tomorrow. It was true there'd be others around, but it wasn't like at school where he was the teacher and she his student—and with other students having the right to expect his full attention. He tried to not anticipate too much as to his relationship with her, yet found himself thinking of how soft that toffee-blond hair looked and what it would feel like should he run his fingers through it.

And there was that slow, sweet smile she'd given him this morning when he'd inquired as to Michael's health, and her actually taking a step toward him.

He marveled at having told her of his dream of becoming a physician. Even his parents didn't know of that, and he couldn't afford to have the powers that be here at the university get wind of it, either! He'd been given his professorship in almost record time, and they obviously expected him to stay.

And perhaps he would.

He'd asked himself already if he might be an education junkie, for he loved learning, was always absorbing facts about subjects as varied as Civil War battles, medical breakthroughs, archaeology and, of course, anything concerning the endocrine system or the mapping of genes.

He also dearly loved sharing that knowledge with others, so yes, he did consider himself to be a good teacher. So why wasn't he experiencing the sense of fulfillment he'd expected by the time he got to this stage of life?

He was almost thirty. Did he want to be alone any longer? He'd held to his conscious decision to not get emotionally involved; he'd never had more money than absolutely necessary and, being a devoted student, had told himself it wouldn't be fair to ask any woman to go through those years with him. He'd weakened just once, but that had been more than enough to keep him single. They were within three weeks of getting married when KathiAnn decided she loved someone else more.

But why in the world was he even thinking such thoughts? Was there something special about Jana that was getting through to him? She was certainly beautiful, but so were a number of other students and acquaintances, and none of them had made him this introspective. Had she said or done anything that set her apart from all others?

Yet when he closed his eyes he could still see her there on the hospital bed, her arm around her little son who'd been so very ill, even in sleep cuddling, holding, loving him. Had something that simple, that basic, brought into focus his need for closeness?

He didn't believe this had anything at all to do with lust, or anything like that, but since then he'd been...

Ray couldn't sort out his thoughts. For someone who prided himself on clear thinking, on being able to concentrate on whatever he chose and push from his consciousness things that would interfere, this was almost intolerable!

He wanted to be with Jana, to talk with her, to get to know her for who she really was—not only as an excellent student and loving mother, but apparently a good friend to the other young mothers with whom she lived, and to at least some of the students at the college.

And her appreciation of and love for Gram was also in her favor.

Both little girls had awakened before Michael, so Jana had already taken them downstairs when she heard her son call for her. She told him to come on downstairs and waited at the foot of the magnificent chestnut staircase for him. She appreciated the fact that she no longer needed to run up and down the stairs so many times, yet it was almost unbelievable how fast the infant stage had passed, as had the toddler one.

The children were playing with trucks and cars in the large front hallway when Ricki came for her daughter. Candi got up and ran to her mother, and then Mary and Michael were doing likewise, all being drawn into the young mother's embrace as she told them, "I missed you kids a whole lot while I was away."

It was a little later that Jana asked, "Are you going to the open house tonight?"

"I think I'll make it—the probable clincher being that they're offering activities for the little ones while we parents wander around."

"It's nice to know that's available, but I expect to keep Michael with me unless he gets too bored or fussy."

"Do you know if Kate will be there?"

"She hadn't made up her mind as of yesterday, but I think she will, in support of Barb, if nothing else."

"Um-hmmm. It's a wonderful opportunity for

families and friends of currently enrolled students and people from the whole area to sample their culinary creations.'' Ricki was gathering Candi's things. ''Anything I can help with here before leaving?''

Jana shook her head. ''Everything seems to be in good condition.'' She followed her friend onto the front porch and waved and called goodbye to Candi three times in response to the little one's over-her-mother's-shoulder farewells.

It was good having all of them so involved in the lives of one another's children, but she was glad Michael would have another male role model on Sunday. It wasn't as though they weren't frequently with some good ones, including Andi's husband and Vanessa's husband, and Gram's sons. However this time Michael would be one-on-one with a man outside Gram's extended family, one not having children of his own.

Not that she knew of, anyway.

She had of course not asked such a thing when he inquired as to her having children other than Michael. But it did concern her that she knew almost nothing of Ray's personal life. *Why am I so intrigued by him, and drawn to him?*

* * *

Jana had not expected to be greeted by a sad-faced clown just inside the food institute's entrance, but apparently he was part of the welcoming committee. She didn't recognize him as Todd until she noted that familiar twinkle in his eyes as he straightened after a pathetically awkward bow before her, resulting in a fake stumble.

She'd instinctively grabbed for his hand with her free one and was relieved when his shuffling, outsize clown shoes were once again beneath him as he pretended to struggle at regaining his balance.

"Welcome, fair lady," he said, then reached with his misshapen-gloved hand for that of her son. "And welcome to you, young Michael."

The child drew back against her shoulder, chin tucked down as he looked at this strange being. Smiling, she withdrew her hand from Todd's. "We thank you for your welcome and have every expectation of enjoying ourselves."

"I'm sure you will, Jana."

He turned to greet the arrivals behind them as she and Gram moved forward. "I'm sorry I couldn't introduce you to Todd Livingston, but this is hardly the time or place."

Gram's eyes were sparkling as much as Todd's had been. "He seems like a fine young man."

"He is, but this is a far different side of him from any I'd seen before. I've known him from being in two of my classes. He's an excellent student and is active in the Christian Club."

"I don't remember their having a clown or anything like that last year."

"They didn't, but Barb did mention that someone from the college had volunteered. They thought prospective students and families might enjoy a touch of something very informal and fun so this wouldn't be seen as just an advertisement for students or a showcase of what the present ones are capable of doing."

They kept meeting and visiting with other friends as they continued through the various areas. Four or five students, spotlessly clothed in white, including those distinctive big-topped chef's hats, were in each room, serving visitors a miscellany of appetizer-or-cocktail-size delicacies.

These ranged from charmingly cut and presented fruits and vegetables to mini French toast, sticky buns and novelty pastries to a great variety of seafood, meat and cheeses.

Gram and Jana found Barb at tables laden with tiny, delicately decorated petit fours and miniature tarts. They had not yet spoken to her when there was a distraction just outside the room and Todd came in with an invisible pet on an extended, fixed-link chain. By holding it with its tip consistently about two feet from the floor, he acted as though a huge, very strong animal was dragging him toward the food-laden tables.

There was laughter and joking as this continued, and Todd took a pratfall before getting up, dusting himself off and handing his end of the leash to Jana!

Gram reached to take wide-eyed Michael into her arms, and Jana tried to act as though attempting with both hands to control the obstreperous pet. Todd hurried in his bumbling manner to the corner of the room and removed what looked like a white tablecloth to expose a large wire cage. He pretended to pull on it with all his might but, not having success, he went to Jana to transfer the leash from her hand to that of a lanky boy in his early teens beside her. Tugging at her hand, he indicated she should help him move the cage.

He whispered without moving his lips, ''Fake it,'' and she did, grunting and straining with the effort, going way beyond what she'd considered her relatively reserved way of doing things.

They worked at pulling and shoving until Jana stopped, stood up straight and flexed her neck and shoulders. Running her right hand across her forehead, she flicked it as though removing perspiration, then raised it to tap a forefinger against her temple and indicate with facial expression her great excitement at having an idea.

She crossed to Gram, lifted her son into her arms and whispered to him, "Would you please help us move this, Michael?"

He looked from her to the cage and nodded, so Jana carried him across the room to hand him to Todd, who set the little boy on the floor beside him. *He looks so tiny there, hardly taller than the cage. Will he be intimidated? Should I tell him what to do?*

But that wasn't necessary, for he put out both hands and started to push while Todd and Jana pretended to be just getting ready to help with this project.

The wire cage started to move, and everyone clapped and cheered for the little fellow, telling him how very strong he was, even more than his mom and the clown! Receiving all this encouragement, he kept on pushing straight across the room, people moving out of his way. It was Barb who brought this to an end by stepping in front of the cage just in time to keep it from crashing into one of the linen-clad, delicacy-laden serving tables.

The approbation continued as Jana picked up her son and, setting him on her shoulder, beckoned Todd to join them as they accepted applause.

And there was Ray, standing just inside the doorway! He, too, had joined in with clapping, but looked somewhat puzzled, and she wasn't at all sure he approved.

Or was there something else?

Chapter Five

~~

She'd never expected to see him here! If she had, she'd possibly not have allowed herself to get drawn into this mummery. *And yet*, she was setting her excited son on the floor and purposely avoiding Ray's eyes as she straightened to her full height. *I've done nothing wrong, and refuse to be apologetic or embarrassed.*

Todd took the chain leash from the teen and pretended to struggle to get the imaginary creature into the cage by first pushing and shoving its head, then its body through the opening. He closed the door and leaned back against it as he struggled to pull a mammoth padlock from his back pocket and secure the cage.

He bowed all the way down to Michael's height to shake his hand before turning to Jana, then gave her a big for-the-audience hug as he whispered for her ears only, "You're one amazing woman! Thanks!"

He pushed the cage into its corner, thrust the "leash" into it, threw kisses to several of the older ladies, including Gram, acknowledged Ray's presence by touching his forearm, and disappeared down the hallway.

Later, while placing two petit fours and a tartlet on her plate, Jana asked Barb, "Did you prepare these?"

"Most of us did some of everything in preparation for tonight, but we four—" Barb motioned toward the other people behind the table "—had the responsibility of seeing that these were as perfect as we could make them."

"They're wonderful, both in appearance and taste!" Gram stated. "We're proud of you, Barb."

"Thanks, Gram. As you know, I delight in beautiful things."

"I'm grateful for that. Someone's got to take care of making beauty, though that's not my strong point."

"Oh, Gram," Barb said, putting an arm around the woman they all loved, "you yourself are beautiful—inside and out."

"I guess I sort of asked for that, didn't I?" She was still smiling when she turned to Jana. "Let's go to the next area and let this overworked girl visit with those she doesn't get to see each day."

Gram did, as usual, stop to speak with various people before they got to the door. Ray was in the line going from table to table, and Jana told herself she had no right to feel a little confused, maybe a tiny bit hurt that he'd done no more to acknowledge her presence than to give a small nod. After all, she'd recently spent an enjoyable evening with him, and he'd since then invited Michael and her to go with him to look at the trains at his railroad station!

Ray deliberately kept talking with the gray-haired couple in front of him, though not really interested in the man's workshop, where he apparently spent most of his time since retiring as a carpenter, or that one of the girls in the second room they'd visited was their granddaughter.

The only woman in this place about whom he

was truly interested had just gone out that door with Michael and Gram—and Ray had done nothing about it! *Why didn't I walk out with them?*

After Ray finished what little food he'd put on his plate, he left the room and looked next door for Jana. He found her and Gram having a serious discussion with one of the white-clad students, but Gram smiled at him in what he considered a welcoming manner. "Isn't this some turnout, Dr. Hawkins?"

"It certainly is!" He was trying for a casual amble in their direction. "I couldn't get here last year, but there are many more people tonight than at the first two."

"Barb Mutchler, who lives with us, was involved with preparations last year, as well—which is why we came then. I'm sure this will not be our last time."

He glanced around the room. "I'm impressed by the fact that each open house gets better." Turning toward Jana, he said, "That was quite a routine you and Michael were involved with."

She laughed aloud. "Had Todd asked beforehand, I'd have refused for sure, for I've never considered doing anything so outlandish. However, the request was sprung on me, and I almost had to do my best.''

"You looked as though you were enjoying yourself."

"I did." Her head was cocked to the side, making her look almost surprised by her own admission. "Maybe I needed it in order for me to break from my stodginess."

"You think you're characterized by stodginess? I can't believe that, Ms. Jana Jenson!"

"Not to argue nor impress by humility, but there are many in your classes who are much more scintillating than I."

"Hmm." He pursed his lips and frowned in mock concentration before stating solemnly, "I can't think of a single one."

Michael was pulling on her skirt. "Up, Mama. I want to see what's on the tables."

But it was Ray who leaned over and lifted the child in his arms. "Is this better, young man?"

A quick up-and-down with his head was Michael's answer to that question before he said, "Can I eat some grapes?"

Ray looked at Jana with raised brows, knowing he wasn't the one to give permission. She nodded. "They do look delicious, but they're so big, and you've eaten so much already that you may take just six of them.''

Ray held him out far enough to pick up the toothpick inserted in each, with the boy counting aloud, "One, two, three, four, five, six.''

He'd placed them on the plate held by his mother but wanted down while eating them. Jana chose several chunks of candied pineapple and mango, a few dates stuffed with nutmeats and two grapes. Ray did likewise, appreciating the fact that they apparently had similar tastes.

They finished the circuit together and went to the lobby, where they stayed long enough for each to get something to drink. When the women said they were leaving right away because Michael was getting sleepy, Ray learned they were parked in the same lot he'd used and said he'd walk them to their car.

His coming tonight had been largely due to this institute's being a branch of the college and his feeling that the different disciplines should support one another with their presence. However, this evening had turned out to be very satisfying.

He carried the tired child across the macadam, realizing that, although he'd never spent much time around small children, it had seemed perfectly natural to lift Michael and hold him while the boy chose those grapes—as right as holding him now.

And this led to the questions he continued asking himself once he'd left Gram and Jana. Were most kids Michael's age so well coordinated? Did they speak as distinctly and count up to six? Would they be as good and as willing to cooperate as this little boy, who had just been so frighteningly ill?

He grunted suddenly, there alone in the front seat of his car. In spite of all his schooling and teaching about endocrinology and genetics and other branches of science, he'd never before seriously thought about what it might be like to have a child of his own.

Saturday was the only day of the week when Jana had no early-morning time crunch, so she'd told herself last night that she'd sleep in. However, habit proving stronger than desire, she was wide-awake before six.

Deciding to roll over and enjoy what she considered a luxury, she pulled the covers over her head. Though sleep didn't come, she went over last evening, still amazed at her unaccustomed participation in Todd's little skit, and thrilled at how willingly Michael had gone along with what was asked of him.

He's not a baby anymore; he's a dear little boy with a desire to please me and others. Michael entered into that with no trace of being a show-off, just willing to do as I requested. She inched the blanket down enough to look across at him in the other bed, lying there on his tummy with arms and legs spread out, face turned toward her but eyes closed as he continued sleeping.

Oh, God, thanks again for making it possible for me to come to Gram's when I had to leave home! Thanks so very much for my Sunday school teacher and pastor for caring enough to make those arrangements—which have to classify as major miracles!

Thank You for seeing Michael through this latest crisis. He was having such a terrible time drawing in each breath, and I was so scared— having that same old fear that maybe he wouldn't make it this time, that You might still be punishing me—that maybe You were going to take him from me after all.

But You were with us all the while! I'm sorry

to have again doubted Your forgiveness. You've promised to give that if I sincerely confess my sins and ask for Your forgiveness and promise to do better, but I obviously need more faith, Lord. Please help me with that—at least having enough so I won't fall apart emotionally, so I can be strong for Michael and others—and myself. My son does need me, almost as much as I need him—and You.

Jana yawned and shifted position, closing her eyes in the effort to entice sleep, but instead found herself again remembering last night.

She'd had such a good time both last night and the visit to the station house! Was it more than a coincidence that Ray had been part of both? She hoped he'd ask her out again—then told herself not to daydream or even think about the professor any more. For all she knew, he might already be involved with some other woman.

Her eyes opened abruptly, and she rolled over on her back to stare at the ceiling. *And why wouldn't he, Jana Jenson? He's good-looking enough to turn any woman's head, and he's got to be very intelligent and well-thought-of to already be a full professor at his age! Who am I, for goodness sake, to think he could care for someone like me?*

She reminded herself that she was quite capable of taking responsibility for herself and her son, or would be when finished with college. But it annoyed her that it wasn't easy to put that man out of her mind and keep him there, for she did like and respect him, and he'd been so generous in bringing that planter for her son.

It was she who must shape up, be realistic, keep romantic fantasies from leading her into daydreams that could never become more than that.

Hearing Gram leave the bathroom, Jana decided she might as well get her shower, then put on jeans and went downstairs instead. "Good morning, Gram. I'm going out and get the lawn mowed before getting cleaned up for the day."

"I'd been standing here looking out the kitchen window, trying to make up my mind as to whether it really needed to be done today or if it could wait till Monday," Gram admitted.

"Then the decision's made," Jana stated, heading for the key rack to pick up keys for the garage and mower. Until the girls came to live with her and having a broken hip a few years ago, Gram had insisted upon doing this, stating that the lawn was too small to warrant investing in a riding mower and that the exercise was good for her.

Since then, however, one of the girls always took care of this responsibility, and as Jana briskly walked behind the mower she planned how to best use the rest of today. Other than spending time with her son, priority must be given to serious studying, for she'd recently been unable to concentrate fully on several subjects.

After returning the mower to the garage, Jana joined the others in the kitchen for breakfast.

"*That* was certainly fast," Gram commended, removing a pancake from the electric griddle.

"With the incentive of eating your pancakes with those I love best in the world," Jana said, standing at the kitchen sink washing her hands, "I wasn't about to fool around out there."

As usual, Gram led in prayer. Then Michael joined in with all of them, "God is great, God is good, and we thank Him for our food. Amen."

Jana had thought about that couplet many times, and she did try to remember to thank God for not only food, but everything. However, while placing two pancakes on her plate and decanting maple syrup over them, she shared her reservations. "Gram, did your kids recite that 'God is great' verse as their prayer when they were little?"

"We used it for the first couple of years when they were very small, then decided they should be thinking of specifics they were thankful for or wanted to bring to God's attention," Gram said.

"Then why aren't we doing that now?" Jana asked.

Gram reached over to cover Jana's hand with hers. "Michael is your son, dear, and I promised myself to try not to interfere in the way you choose to raise him."

"Oh, Gram!" She felt tears forming in her eyes, but continued, "Don't you realize that I want your input? That I *need* it?"

"Times have changed so much since my children were little, Jana, and there are different ways of doing things. It's only right for you to have the say-so as to rearing your son."

"But I'm still feeling my way and need guidance! I'm an only child, and my parents' major goal was for me to be a credit to *them*. And even at that I failed." She remembered all too well how she'd failed by getting pregnant, then by being unwilling to have that abortion they'd insisted upon. They considered the second immeasurably more unforgivable than the first.

"You're an excellent mother, you really are." Gram squeezed the hand she'd not relinquished. "You did make a mistake, but how can you possibly look at this remarkable son of yours and associate him with failure?"

"You do have a way of giving a different perspective on things, Gram," Jana informed her. "Thanks."

Gram picked up her fork and cut off a bite-size piece of syrup-soggy pancake. "But to get back to what started this discussion, Jana, I wholeheartedly approve of your recommendation about prayers."

Jana decided to try for another equally important agreement. "*And* my recommendation about giving advice when I need it?"

"You'd be sorry if I agreed to that!" Gram chuckled. "When I might think you need it could be totally different from when you do."

"But that's when I'm most likely to be needing you. I'm not saying I'll always agree, but we could at least discuss matters."

AnnaMae called after breakfast, and invited

Michael to come to her apartment for the rest of the morning and stay for lunch. After she and her daughter, Mary, came to pick him up, Gram was about to leave for her daily walk. Jana asked, "Since Michael's not here to slow you down, how about my going with you today?"

"I'd love that!"

"Even if I have trouble keeping up with you by the end of your three miles?"

"Even should that happen—which, incidentally, I don't expect." They were starting down the front walk, and Gram glanced in both directions. "You call it, Jana. Which route shall we take?"

It really made no difference to her, but she motioned toward the right. "There's nothing I need from a store, so let's go this way." The day was balmy, temperature still near seventy, although the morning news had predicted afternoon temperatures into the upper eighties.

Friends and acquaintances working in flower beds or doing other outdoor tasks called greetings but remained where they were. "This has got to be a record, Gram. We've walked at least ten blocks and haven't stopped to visit even once!"

Gram's familiar chuckle sounded. "Sorta nice,

isn't it? I love talking with people, as you know all too well, but it's good to stride along with you today—just the two of us."

"It is indeed. And I was just thinking how interesting it is that I have such a sense of companionship and communication with you that silences are as satisfying as conversation."

"That's one of the things I missed most after my husband was killed." Her voice was very soft. "But I didn't mention it to others, afraid they wouldn't understand. Everyone sympathized about the physical loss, not having Phil beside me at home or at church or anywhere. Not being able to do things with him."

There was another pause. "When I was most heartsick of all was when I was alone and had an idea or item I just had to share with him—not necessarily a big problem or concern or even a major blessing, maybe just the first violet of spring, or a spectacularly beautiful sunset, or perhaps something like that little girl over there being pushed on the swing by her father—and it would almost overwhelm me to know I could never, ever do that again. And I'd stand there, feeling like I'd become half a person, since God had truly made us one."

Jana reached for Gram's hand. "I'm sorry."

Gram came to a complete stop on the sidewalk in front of the grade school. "But there are important truths that I keep reminding myself of, Jana. The first is that I was blessed beyond measure by having loved and been loved by Phil.

"And the second's just as important—God had by that time already given me a loving family, those who were born into or married into it. And wonderful friends.

"And then you and the other girls came into my home and my heart."

"Thanks, Gram." Jana could only whisper those words.

Gram cleared her throat and started walking again, this time not as briskly. "I want to tell you again, dear, how I admire your keeping on keeping on. Though you didn't have any support from your family when you needed it, you've pitched in here and become an integral part of our family."

"I love your family."

"And the feeling's returned in full."

"I am so blessed, Gram, by having a second family, with you and the other girls."

Chapter Six

Gram and Jana talked about many things after that and were home in what seemed record time. Two messages had been left on the answering machine, the first a prayer request from their next-door neighbor, Gin Redding, for her daughter, who'd been taken to the hospital with chest pain.

The second was for Jana, from Ray Hawkins, asking that she return his call.

Has he changed his mind about tomorrow? Jana wondered. But then she chided herself for thinking so negatively. After all, there could be another reason.

And maybe we shouldn't even be going with

him to see the trains. I've done almost no dating, and thought that was best, especially for Michael. And I really don't know Ray—Professor Hawkins—at all well. He seems nice as a person, as well as brilliant as my teacher, but my first responsibility has got to be my son—which reminds me that I've already told Michael about where we planned to go, and he's so very excited.

Ray answered the phone on the first ring, and his upbeat voice inquired as to her having a good Saturday. After a little more small talk, he said, "I've been wondering if you'd be interested in going earlier tomorrow. If we left around eleven, that would give us plenty of time to go somewhere for dinner before seeing the trains."

"That does sound like an interesting possibility," Jana said. "But Michael and I always go to Sunday school and church with Gram, and we don't get home till noon or a little later."

"Oh." His voice sounded less enthusiastic, then became almost conspiratorial. "What are the chances of playing hooky this one time?"

"Not very good. In fact—" she allowed herself to give a little laugh "—not good at all. We're always in church on Sunday, all of us together. It's an important part of our week."

"Well, it seemed worth a try."

He'd kept his voice light, as though it didn't really matter, but she couldn't respond in like fashion. "I realize Michael's too young to recognize on his own that tomorrow is Sunday, but it's important to me to be there. And I hope he'll soon grasp the fact that this is what he and I do on the first day of the week." *Does what I just said sound as sanctimonious to him as it almost does to me?*

"Well, okay."

She waited, wondering if he might choose to cancel their afternoon together. She heard what sounded like a small sigh, "Then I'll see you according to our original schedule."

"We'll look forward to that."

Barb had come in during this exchange and stood with a half smile and a thumbs-up. "Way to go, Jana!"

"Did I come across as preachy? Holier than thou?"

Gram looked about to say something, but Barb beat her to it. "Not to me, it didn't."

"I could have just said no without explaining, but…" She wasn't sure how to finish that.

"If this should turn out to be just a casual,

second-time-only get-together or last time of being with him, it probably wouldn't matter very much,'' Gram hypothesized. ''But if you're hoping he'll continue to be part of your life, it really does.''

''I don't know him well enough to hope that. I did enjoy being with him at the train meeting, yet he didn't seem overly cordial when we ran into him at your open house, Barb. Not until the end, anyway, when he walked us to the car.''

She realized they must have been aware of that, too, for neither responded.

Ray set the phone down slowly and stood a moment with his hand on it. *As though,* he scoffed, *I were still keeping in contact with her.* He wished he knew more of her background and what she was like, but wouldn't ask anyone even if he could.

He didn't always trust his instincts concerning women, couldn't, actually—not since shortly before finishing his doctorate. He tried to clear that from his mind, the remembrance of KathiAnn. It was still painfully humbling that it wasn't until he asked her to become his wife just as soon as they got their degrees that she informed him she was already married!

He'd of course realized from her luxury car and apartment that she had no financial worries, but she'd told him that her parents were well-to-do. He'd had no suspicions whatsoever as to her already being wedded to a much older and extremely successful orthopedic surgeon whom she had no intention of divorcing.

He later learned that her frequent weekend visits to "her ailing mother" had been one of the many lies he'd believed. The one good thing from this was that KathiAnn's duplicity had made him wary of opening his heart or letting down his guard as far as relationships were concerned.

However, he still considered himself to be more astute than some of his colleagues, several of whom had made incredibly bad choices. There'd been that incident four or five years ago when Jack Plummer, in the English department, had that affair with one of the freshmen girls.

And the following year Jeff Pysher, assistant dean of men, found himself involved in a paternity suit. As a result, he'd lost his wife, his three kids, his home and his position at the school.

These scandals led the university to strengthen their sexual harassment policy, the resultant doc-

ument being considered by some almost a no-
fraternization policy, though it actually wasn't. It
was enough, however, to make Ray wonder if
he'd be taking a chance continuing to see Jana.

The problem was that he really liked her and
wanted to get to know her better. He figured that
their being together should be safe as long as he
was careful where he took her—to always be
around others, like at Gram's, or in restaurants
or with his railroad friends.

*At least I'm not young and foolish anymore;
I'm sure I can control my hormones and my
heart. I'm not going to live in fear, and cancel
my get-together with Jana and Michael. Perhaps
I should, but I do want to be the one to take them
to see our trains.*

Jana had gone to Sunday school from the time
she was three years old because her maternal
grandmother came for her each week. Those sessions had been wonderful, the teachers loving
and seeming to have unlimited patience with
their charges as they told stories and had crafts
and activities and sang songs.

Church, however, was something to be gotten
through, a situation about which she was now

sorry. She wished Grandma DeWise were still living so she could tell her so.

By the time Jana was about twelve, she'd stated that she'd had it with sitting through such a boring hour and understood the feelings of her parents, who'd come to that decision for themselves before she was born—though they did have her baptized as an infant.

So the only time she'd heard Dr. Bertolli preach or expound after that was at her grandmother's funeral, the year Jana got pregnant. That was one service she'd never forget. The church was almost full, many people she'd never met or heard of having come from all over to honor and mourn the woman who'd apparently helped so many in all sorts of ways.

She must have been a lot like Gram, but all I ever thought about was her loving concern for me—and I took that for granted, having no conception of how precious love is.

These thoughts kept running through her mind on Sunday morning when she should have been paying more attention to Pastor Harriman's sermon. Today's was based on a text in Philippians about finding or claiming joy in any circumstance.

Certainly she'd found no joy when she was in trouble at home—finding herself pregnant at age sixteen and being given the ultimatum of getting rid of the child within her. It was then, desperate for someone to take her side, that she'd gone to Dr. Bertolli.

And he, having met Gram and knowing of her plans to help those in this situation, helped make the arrangements that had brought Jana to Sylvan Falls.

Without planning to do so, Jana reached over and took Gram's hand. The older woman didn't look surprised, just smiled at her and held it snugly there for that last minute or two until the sermon was over and it was time to open their hymnals and join in the final singing.

Jana left the pew as quickly as possible, hurrying to get her son, not only because of eagerness to get home and eat and be ready for Ray's arrival, although that could be part of it, she admitted to herself. It was mostly because her thoughts during church had made her realize once again how very much she loved Michael. And of how grateful she was to have not given in to her parents' ultimatum.

Jana spoke briefly with the two women in the

church's preschool area, then took Michael with her to the sanctuary, rejoicing again at seeing him relate so well to all those who took time to talk to him and reach out and touch him. She felt the smile come to her face as she thought that maybe God might have this same warm feeling when people here on earth reached out to His children. In love.

She was sure He did.

If Michael's lunch was eaten a bit more slowly than usual, it was due to his chattering about Sunday school and church time. He was with Deborah, Candace and Mary most of his waking hours, and got to see his church friends only on Sunday, so he had to share in detail what they had played and done this morning.

Jana had changed into casual wear before eating and was upstairs getting her son into shorts and a T-shirt when Barb called, "He's here, Jana. He just parked out front."

"We'll be right down," she assured, and they were descending the lower half-flight of stairs as Ray walked onto the porch.

Seeing him through the screen door, Michael piped up. "We're comin'!"

Ray's smile for the child became even bigger for Jana. "I hope I'm not too early?"

She shook her head. "You're right on time."

"Ready to leave?"

"Yes, we are." She picked up the child's car seat from where she'd left it beside the door, and they walked to Ray's vehicle, each adult holding one of Michael's hands.

Ray opened the back door and reached for the car seat. "I'll take care of this if you give instructions."

"Some are rather tricky, but this one's fairly simple," she said, setting it in place. "You just do this and this." She secured the car's seat belt through the seat. "Then you pick up the little guy, set him in it and fasten his restraint."

"It looks simple enough even for me." Ray was grinning as he opened her front door at the same time she closed the back one.

She sat down and he pulled the shoulder belt out far enough to allow him to reach across and fasten it. Her breath caught for a moment. This was the closest contact they'd ever had.

"There!" He backed away, his lips for that split second only an inch or two from hers.

He closed her door, and as he walked around

the front of the car she struggled to control that faster-than-usual pulse rate of which she'd suddenly become conscious. *Stop being so ridiculous!* she scolded. *You're no longer a carefree teen who can spend her time fantasizing about a charming, handsome young prince who's mad about you and here to carry you away to a life of trouble-free happiness!*

Watch it, buddy! Ray cautioned himself as he slid under the steering wheel and slammed the door. *I'm not sure you should have fastened that seat belt, leaning across her like that, being so close, so almost intimate.*

But she was looking at Michael, answering something he'd apparently asked—something Ray had not heard. Their gaze met as he looked at her while starting the car; she was turning to face frontward, murmuring, "He's been putting on a good act of being full of energy, but that thumb in his mouth's a giveaway."

"He's over the effects of the croup?"

"Pretty much, but it always takes awhile to get back to normal."

"Is he more fussy?"

"Not as much as I'd probably be if I couldn't

breathe and felt that rotten. He's so patient that I have no right to feel sorry for myself when being up with him night after night.''

He'd started to pull into the street but gave another quick glance in her direction. ''I didn't realize it was night after night. I thought he just got sick the night you took him to the hospital.''

''This time was like that, but sometimes—perhaps he may have a bit of a cold or been exposed to one of the yet unknowns he could be allergic to—whatever the cause, we may be up one night after another. And also have a humidifier running in our room many nights.''

''You share a room?'' Ray asked. *This is none of my business, but I'm usually not thinking of mothers and children sleeping in the same room—for that matter, I normally don't wonder about how people sleep.*

''At first it was a convenience, with my nursing him, and his crib taking little space. At that time all the second-floor rooms were occupied, but we later moved into the front room with twin beds. He's an excellent roommate when well, drifting off even if I'm working at my desk or lying in bed studying—and he sleeps throughout the night.''

This is the first time I've been on a date—though this isn't a real date, of course—and discussed the woman's sleeping arrangements! There's not an ounce of self-consciousness in Jana. He found he liked that about her—he liked her.

He mentioned that his interest in trains had been with him as long as he could remember. "When I was small, I had an elderly great-uncle who as a younger man had been a conductor on the Pennsylvania Railroad. I guess some people were tired of his stories about the good old days when most people went places and shipped things by rail, but I was enthralled.

"One of my most vivid early memories is of Uncle Jake taking me inside a huge black steam engine. I got to talk to the engineer and put my hand on the throttle. It *seems* as though the train was operational—but may not have been, since I was allowed to ring the bell and blow the whistle."

That memory always made him smile. "I was hooked from that day on—have been a railroad nut ever since."

"And the station you're taking me to—how did you get involved there?"

He shifted position. "I was at loose ends when arriving here. I didn't know a soul except for those who'd interviewed me at the university and took me out for dinner. Then I heard about this station being open for at least a couple of hours each Sunday afternoon from late spring till early fall, so I checked it out the very first weekend after coming to this area."

Jana seemed genuinely interested, so he continued. "I loved every thing about it, especially the enthusiasm of those working at restoration. We were kindred spirits, and even that first day I couldn't resist helping remove rust from the boxcar they were working on."

He chuckled. "I managed to ruin a perfectly good pair of slacks, but found something I enjoy far more than knocking a little white ball over mowed hills and hollows or trying to get fish to choose my lure."

"And you have something to show for all your effort."

She'd sounded approving. "There's years of work ahead of us, for we keep getting involved with different projects, like their having bought old rails and ties shortly before I got here and lugging them here to build a new siding.

"I got to help with the final stages of that, and we've spruced up a couple of the cars. Nothing's yet in near-new condition, but I'll admit to being proud of having my hands in so many of the accomplishments."

"That *would* give tremendous satisfaction," Jana said.

Ray was pleased she understood his fascination with trains.

She reached to flip down the visor in front of her and adjust it so she could use the mirror, but he appreciated finding that this woman wasn't checking her makeup or fussing with her hair or practicing a smile. She was checking on her son, and reported, "He's already asleep."

Ray glanced at Michael just as the little fellow's hand was sliding across his chest to rest on his lap. His head had tilted into the slight angle of his seat's back, and his eyes were closed. "I suppose that's the best thing for him right now."

"Yes, it is."

"Is he apt to be grumpy when he wakes up?" He remembered too late that he'd already asked if Michael had been fussy since being so sick, but it did seem to him that an awful lot of kids out with their parents were like that!

"I can't promise he won't be. That would be asking for trouble, wouldn't it?" She laughed. "But he normally has a wonderful disposition, even when first waking up."

Another quick glance showed her sitting there, apparently completely relaxed with him, head leaned against the top of the seat. She glanced at him, a half smile on her face, beautiful dark blue eyes meeting his gaze as she said, "I meant to introduce you to Barb. She's the one who's a student at the food institute. She called upstairs when she saw you parking, but I didn't see her when Michael and I came down."

"I caught a glimpse of someone leaving the back of the hallway when I was coming up the steps."

"She's my very best friend—well, she and Gram—and we all live together."

"It's just the four of you?"

"At night, but it's not at all like that during the day!"

She quickly moved on to a different topic. "The people I met with you the other night seemed very pleasant. Are they from all walks of life?"

"And how! We range from a medical doctor to a woman in housekeeping at the hospital, from a teacher at the food institute, which is one of the ways I learned about that open house, to a young man who clears tables at McDonald's. There's even one of the gofers on the maintenance crew at the college—as well as an egghead like me. We all get along very well."

Jana asked questions about certain individuals she'd met, and he cheerfully responded. She finally admitted, "I'm glad you just introduced us by name, not title. I'd have been intimidated!"

"Only for a little bit, Jana, but I didn't want you uncomfortable at all."

"I wasn't, at least not much. And your friends, your co-workers and others, couldn't have been more gracious, more welcoming."

"They were more than just interested, however." This time his sideways glance was a bit longer, and the corner of his mouth quirked a bit. "That was the first time I'd brought a woman with me, so they were curious."

"Oh!" Jana wasn't certain if that had been vocalized or said in her thoughts but, hoping for the latter, she remained silent.

Perhaps he guessed that his comment made her

uncomfortable, for he went back to specifics as to the work he'd done, and she was more than ready to go along with that.

It seemed to take almost no time before they arrived at the station. Her interest was primarily on the mammoth steam engine and other rolling stock, not as much on the refurbished building. But then she realized he'd said nothing more, probably waiting for her to do or say something. She turned as much as her seat belt allowed. "Michael, dear, it's time to wake up now. We're here at the railroad."

He stretched, and his thumb returned to his mouth, but she had to be more detailed. "We're here with the trains, dear. Would you like to go see them?"

His eyelids flickered, then opened. Sitting up erectly, he looked around with interest as his thumb left his mouth. "Yeah! *In* the train."

She looked at Ray with raised brows, and he responded while parking. "That's an excellent idea, Michael! We're going into the engine and the sleeper and the boxcar for sure."

The child was unsuccessfully attempting to re-lease himself from the restraints, so as soon as the vehicle came to a stop Jana got out of the front seat and helped Michael from his. He started running as soon as his feet were on the ground, but she caught hold of the crossed straps on the back of his overalls. "Remember the rules, Michael! You must stay with me, not run ahead."

He looked from her to the engine and back again. "Let's hurry!"

"A child after my own heart!" Ray grinned at the impatient youngster and reached for his hand. "If your mother takes hold of your other one, I'll bet we can get over there real fast."

How nice of him! "We're both eager to see everything." She did as suggested, and when they got to the huge engine, it was easy to swing Michael up to the high first step.

He let Michael lead the way into the cab, and Jana wondered if Ray was deliberately doing for this youngster what his uncle had for him, for he couldn't have been kinder to her son. Answering each question, no matter how small or seemingly irrelevant, he explained in simple terms whatever Michael wanted to know. Jana would also have liked to ask a few, but didn't. This was Michael's time to learn not only about a steam engine, but also about a gentle, kind man who was so willingly giving of his time and knowledge.

He couldn't be putting on an act for her benefit, could he? That thought was unworthy of her—and of him! He was not talking down to Michael; not being *professorial*; they were interacting, relating with one another.

She tried to put herself in Michael's position, but found that impossible. The engine seemed big to her; how mammoth it must be for him! And the whistle he blew and the bell he rang sounded awfully loud to her, but just right to him!

Thinking of it in the opposite way was almost harder to do, although most inviting. Michael was sitting on the professor's lap, with the man's arm around him and his hand on the child's at times as he showed what the engineer would be doing in such-and-such a situation.

What would it be like to have his arm around her, his hand on hers, his face that near as he explained?

Drawing in her breath sharply, she stood more erect, and Ray glanced at her. "Problem, Jana?"

She felt increased warmth in her cheeks and glanced away for a moment, afraid he might have read her thoughts. "Not at all, but I've never been in one of these, either, and it's a bit overwhelming."

"I was afraid you might be bored or something."

He was beaming, and she suspected she might be doing the same thing. She didn't meet his gaze for more than a second as she deliberately, obviously, examined her surroundings. "How could anyone be bored with all this?"

Michael saved the situation by asking, "What's *this* thing for?"

And Dr. Raymond Hawkins explained yet another of the mysteries of this big black engine.

What a good man he is, Jana thought, touched by the sight of Michael and Ray interacting so well together.

Chapter Seven

"We were incredibly lucky to get this," Ray told her. "The last engine I know of that came up for sale in so-called excellent condition had an asking price of a cool million."

"A million *dollars?*"

"The owner didn't get that on his first try, and I don't know if he has, or will, but it's probably worth it. However, this one, rusty and almost forgotten, was on a siding in one of the old lumber ghost towns until Tony Chalmers, a railroader from way back, rescued it maybe thirty years ago, paying next to nothing for it, by the way.

"Fortunately, there was still usable track there at the time, so he was able to get it out, then ended up paying rent to park it somewhere. He did some work on it and promised himself to some day finish the job, but after a massive heart attack about ten years ago, Tony realized he'd never get done what was needed.

"So he offered it to our group for one dollar. Well, one dollar from each member, actually, for he wanted to be sure that, as he said, 'Everyone will have a stake in it.' And he made two other stipulations. It must eventually be restored, and it must never be sold."

"That seems like a very big promise to make. How could they make such a contract? Perhaps they'd disband or something."

"Exactly!" He gave a crooked smile. "Even though they really wanted it, they weren't sure they could keep that promise, but did sign documents stating that, should we cease functioning, this would be given to some other deserving railroad museum or organization."

"What a perfect solution!" *And your smiling enthusiasm is also perfect.*

"We think so. And ya know? There's been an added blessing to making that agreement. This particular item—" slowly moving his palm up-hand to encompass the piece of Americana

"—has become a representation of all we stand for, the solidarity and purpose of our group."

Jana felt privileged to have this man share these things with her and listened carefully as he continued. "The untold hours—the years of dedicating ourselves to making it the best we're capable of—have helped many to discover qualities in ourselves we never knew we had. We've spent countless hours working together, and sometimes even by ourselves, doing strenuous work the likes of which we'd probably not put into anything that belonged to one of us personally.

"We share ideas and friendships, and I've come to know a number of these people better than any of my colleagues."

"Isn't it marvelous how working together toward a goal binds people together?" Jana's words had been spoken almost reverently, with gratitude, for she was realizing that she'd experienced this same sort of thing ever since coming to Sylvan Falls.

The afternoon went by rapidly as they spent another half hour exploring the steam engine before Ray showed Jana and Michael a Pullman railroad car and then a diesel engine. Later, as they pulled into the Old Station Restaurant, Ray said, "I'm not sure we'll get to sit in the restored dining car. I understand that's often reserved months in advance for weddings, birthday celebrations or other special occasions."

"Have you been here before?" Jana asked.

"Several times. Thus far I've been lucky as to seating—so I hope that holds good for today, as well."

Since they'd arrived early for the usual dinner hour, there'd been only a few waiting to be seated, so it was after they'd been led to a table in the dining car that Jana took her son with her to the bathroom to wash up.

They'd been back with Ray for less than five minutes when a very long northbound train raced by, causing the salt and pepper shakers to rattle against one another. At home, the children were seldom allowed to leave the table until they finished eating, but this time Jana joined Michael as he raced for the window and stood there, entranced.

"All gone," he sighed when the only thing left was the decreasing rumble of steel on steel.

She rumpled his hair. "But wasn't it great?"

"Uh-huh." He willingly walked to their table

with her, and spent the next several minutes excitedly telling Ray about what he'd just seen.

"And did you notice it was a diesel engine pulling all those cars?" Ray asked. He had told Michael earlier that diesel engines were stronger than steam engines and they could pull bigger loads. However, Michael favored the steam engines since his picture books featured them.

A short-lived cloud covered Michael's face before dissipating in the thrill of having watched that train. "Uh-huh. It did 'most as good as a steam engine."

She grinned at the man across from her. "Tenacious little mind, isn't it?"

Ray laughed aloud. "It is, indeed!" But then he spoke to her son quite seriously. "I respect your loyalty to the steam engine, Michael. More power to you!" And he reached out to shake the child's hand, which looked tiny within that large, strong one.

Jana cleared her throat, surprised at the realization of its being unshed moisture from her eyes that caused the thickening. *Yes, this man is a fine male role model for my son. Even should it prove to be for just this one day, it's been good for Michael to get to know him.*

It was Ray who brought up the matter of her son's usual bedtime, and Jana was almost sorry to tell him it was already upon them. They'd dawdled over the meal, enjoying the food, but getting to know one another better seemed even more enjoyable. They were nearly ready to leave when the waiter told them the southbound train would be coming within the next ten or fifteen minutes, and brought drink refills as they waited to see the train pass by before going out into the much cooler evening.

The sun was setting, but Jana wasn't consciously aware of that until they were heading for home on country roads. "This has been a truly special day," she murmured, resting her head back against the seat.

"It has been for me, too," Ray commented. "And I believe it was for your son, as well."

She turned toward him. "Michael didn't miss a thing, did he?"

The glow of early evening highlighted Ray's smile. "I don't know what it could have been."

"I hope he'll remember at least some of it."

"Even if it's only in having an undying love of trains."

"But I hope it will be much more than that."

She didn't admit even to herself why she'd said that.

"You sound wistful."

His voice had been very soft, and he glanced her way again. Searching through memories, she came upon some that were very good. "I have some recollections of when I wasn't yet in school, things like climbing in bed with my mother and father in the early morning and their letting me snuggle there between them. And of going with my mother to visit her mother, whom I dearly loved."

She stopped there, embarrassed by having shared such uninteresting-to-anyone-else nostalgia. She sat up straight and said, "I'm glad Michael's getting to build a reservoir of good memories. They're important to hold on to, to drink from when things later in life aren't always that way."

He said nothing, perhaps waiting for her to continue, but she wasn't about to. She turned around enough in her seat to see that Michael's thumb was in his mouth. "How about our singing a song, Michael?"

As the little hand lowered, she whispered for

Ray's ears only, "I hope you don't mind, but he was almost asleep back there."

"I don't mind at all." He gave her that grin she was coming to cherish. "In fact, I look forward to it."

In the back seat Michael sang. "Peter, Peter, Pumpkin eater, had a wife...." Jana's voice joined Michael's for that short nursery song, then went on suggesting and singing others.

Michael was yawning by the time they were approaching Sylvan Falls, so she encouraged him to stay awake a little longer by suggesting, "Maybe you can tell Gram about being inside the train."

"I'll tell her 'bout being in the engine," he corrected.

"Great! She'll be happy to hear that. Gram likes engines."

"And the trains that went past where we ate!"

"That, too, Michael."

He chattered about things he'd tell Gram, even while Jana was saying to Ray, "Thank you for a lovely afternoon and evening. We both enjoyed them very much."

Ray was pulling to the curb in front of their house, and she thought that was why he hesitated in making a polite response. What he ended up saying was far different from what she expected. "May I ask a favor, Jana?"

She nodded, and he shifted position a bit before saying, "I, too, enjoyed the day very much, and certainly have no objection to your talking to your gram or your friend Barb about it.

"However, I'd appreciate your not telling your college or other friends about our being together."

She sucked her breath in harshly, and the contented mood of a moment before evaporated, leaving an empty pit in its place, a matching one to that left by her father's emphatic prediction the last time they'd spoken. *No decent man will ever want to be seen with you!*

She reached for the door handle as she spoke clearly, distinctly. "As you wish, Professor Hawkins. I shall do as you request."

He reached for her hand, but it was yanked away as she left the car and slammed the door in one fluid movement and began to open the rear one. He was unable to exit until a slowly moving car coming down the street finally passed and by the time he hurriedly came around the rear of his car, he was repeating what he'd already said. "Jana, wait, please wait. I'm sorry I worded it like that. I should have explained why I had to say that."

She already had the safety straps released and was taking her son into her arms, holding him close and turning away as though using her own body to protect him from Ray.

He found himself begging, "Let me help you... please wait and talk."

"If you really wish to give assistance, you may bring Michael's car seat to the porch." She was halfway to the steps when she added without so much as turning around, "Just set it on the porch as you leave."

"You're not being fair, Jana! There's a good reason...." She was already to the steps. She was leaving him, and for her sake Ray must not go charging up there after her or shouting so all the neighbors would hear. Glancing around, he became aware of people sitting on the porch just beyond this one.

He was still fumbling to release Michael's seat from its restraint when the porch door slammed shut. Feeling like a very obvious, bumbling fool, he carried the car seat onto the porch and set it beside the door. *I can't leave like this—but can't force my way in, either, and I can't stand here knocking on her door or ringing the bell.*

With her neighbors sitting there in the semi-darkness, undoubtedly watching his every movement, he could do nothing but turn and, straight-backed and with steady tread, go down those steps and down the walk and around the car and drive home.

He'd seldom felt this low in his entire life.

I'll let Michael do the telling, Jana decided as she entered the house. *If I don't, I'll break down and cry, and I certainly don't want to trouble Gram and Barb.*

Michael ran into the living room, and Gram greeted him with a big smile and the beginning of a question. "Did you like—"

"I was up in the great big black steam engine, Gram!" He raised his arms and was lifted onto the comfortable lap of this woman he loved so much. "And I blew the whistle real loud, and rang the bell!"

Gram had smiled at Jana as she entered, but then gave the child full attention, asking questions and listening to a recital of his time at the station house and of watching the trains go by.

Jana went to the kitchen and got a glass of water, grateful that Barb must have gone on upstairs for the night—or perhaps was out. At the moment, Jana wasn't sure she could keep from falling apart if either woman asked about her day, about where they'd gone to eat or how the evening had gone.

The coldness of the drink helped a little in releasing that tenseness, that almost-choking feeling in her throat, and her standing here, alone, for a minute or two gave her a little more calmness, enough that she thought she could get through going into the living room.

Forcing pretend cheerfulness into her manner and voice, she joined the others, Gram obviously reveling in Michael's account of his day. "You can tell her just one more thing, darling, then it's off to bed for you," Jana told him.

"But, Mama!" It was a heartfelt protest. "There's so much more to tell."

"Well, maybe two things then, but that's all for tonight." She smiled at him, which helped at least a little to melt that icy feeling in her chest. "The rest will have to wait until you get up in the morning."

"But…"

"Better tell her those two things right away."
She took another step toward him. "Otherwise,
my love, it's off to bed right now."

He drew in a deep breath, turned to Gram and
told about the big bed way up high in the Pullman car, which had been converted to a bunk-
house for workers—and, surprising his mother,
the second important item was about the interesting stones in the roadway, which he illustrated
by reaching into his pocket for a handful of peb-
bles she'd not even noted his picking up.

Barb came to the door of her room as Jana and
Michael reached the top of the stairs. "Did you
two have a wonderful time?"

Jana chose to let her son answer for both of
them, and he did that in great detail as Barb followed them across the broad hallway and sat on
Michael's bed as his mother got him ready for
the night. "It's a fascinating place, Barb," Jana
finally said. "I think you'd enjoy seeing it."

"I probably would, but didn't you mention
once that your dad also liked trains? Maybe you
come by your interest naturally."

"Perhaps." Jana raised her brows as she
glanced toward her friend. "However, consider-

ing the circumstances, it could be in spite of that.''

There was an answering nod, showing Barb understood, but the subject was dropped as Barb returned to her conversation with Michael, which continued until she joined them for their nightly prayers.

Jana tucked Michael into bed and kissed him, then, telling Barb she was exhausted and about to call it a night, she returned to the bathroom and changed into a nightgown.

Sleep did not come, although she turned and tossed, trying to find a more comfortable position. She knew all too well that it was her internal discomfort and pain causing her inability to drop off.

Was it never going to end, this insecurity and having to pay for being an unwed single mother? Was she never to know the love and unqualified respect and devotion of a good man?

She still had some studying to do for one of her classes the next day, but had anticipated getting up early enough in the morning to work on it. However, around twelve-fifteen she turned on her bedside light, adjusted her pillows and tried to focus all her attention on the assignment.

She only partially succeeded, but by two-thirty, hoping she was prepared for the pop quiz the teacher might give, she finally slept.

Ray, too, had trouble getting to sleep. If only he'd approached that request of his differently—but he'd never have expected such a dramatic reaction on Jana's part!

Why had she reacted like that, not letting him explain his reasons for saying those words, and what he'd meant by them?

As good a time as they'd had all afternoon and evening, he'd assumed she realized he liked and respected her. And her son had proved to be delightful, a definite plus to their visiting where so much of Ray's free time and energy was expended.

To be fair about it, however, he had to consider that there was no reason for her to be aware of the university's policy, so maybe, once she cooled off enough to let him tell her about it, she'd understand the difficulties he might have if word got around that he'd taken her, one of his female students, out not only once, but twice!

I should have known better! But he admitted to himself he'd deliberately asked her out in spite of the fact that he *did* know better. And there was always the chance that he'd pay for that weakness, that stupidity. Even being interrogated about it would make him feel preadolescent.

What was most surprising, almost appalling, was his realization that the thought of not being with her again upset him greatly.

He'd worked very hard to get where he was. He'd forgone joining fraternities or trying out for the college basketball team, though he'd led his high school team to major wins and awards. He'd knocked himself out to consistently remain at or near the top of each class, had assisted science professors in their research and did some of his own and still wrote and rewrote papers, a number of them published.

What was wrong with him that he'd risk losing all that because of an interest in some beautiful college junior who was in one of the classes that he, a full professor no less, was teaching?

Everything within him, intellectually speaking, resisted admitting that he'd been so hurt by KathiAnn's duplicity that he was wary about trusting anyone. He'd made a conscious decision not to readily open his heart to any woman until he was sure it was safe to do so.

And so, in the middle of that almost sleepless night, Professor Raymond Hawkins resolved to keep his thoughts and dreams where they belonged, on his professional future. He had managed to do that previously, so he could certainly do it now!

Chapter Eight

Jana deliberately arrived at the classroom just a minute or two before the session was set to begin, and was able to walk in with several others she knew well enough to easily speak with. Peripheral vision assured her that Ray was already behind the big table and that he seemed to be looking in her direction, but she continued speaking with one of the girls and sat near the back of the room beside her.

Class started right on time, and she supposed his teaching was as good as always, but today she did not enjoy it. Oh, she took notes and grasped the meaning of what he was saying and wrote down the next assignment, but she experienced no joy.

She resented that it should be this way. She'd always liked this class, but not today. She usually kept her gaze fixed on a speaker's face, but that was almost too painful, seeing the play of expressions as he tried to make his lessons interesting to everyone.

He made a joking reference to something and others laughed, but she couldn't. Life was not the same, not since last night. What did he know or think he knew of her that made him unwilling to have others be aware of her having been with him?

The most confusing part of this whole thing was that he'd known about her having a son before asking her to go with him that very first time and had actually met Michael at the hospital. Was his bringing that gift to her son only an apology for embarrassing her during class?

If that was it, he need not have invited her to that meeting and both her and Michael to see the trains yesterday!

He must have noted that she wore no rings, which should have registered as her not being married—though it wouldn't have indicated if she ever had been.

What was it?

She caught herself frowning with confusion and probably having missed some point he'd just made. She glanced at the wall clock and sighed. There were still a good twenty minutes to get through!

She forced her wayward thoughts into order and concentrated on what he was saying, but she wished she could leave before he excused the class. When that time finally came, she did not go up the aisle between the chairs, then turn toward the door, but crossed toward the inner wall, walked with Linda and left the room—feeling almost as though she was escaping.

So why don't I feel good about it? Hurrying to talk with Todd, she made sure she didn't give herself a chance to answer that question, but said, "Yes, I plan to stay for the noon meeting," when he asked, as always, about that.

He beamed at her. "Great! Lizbet Ross will be speaking, and she always has a meaningful message."

"I haven't heard her, but will look forward to it."

She'd expected him to go in another direction, but instead he sauntered along with her, asking, "What did you do over the weekend?"

She shrugged. "There's always a lot of things to be taken care of."

"Nothing different or unusual?"

Does he know? Has he heard something about where I went and with whom? "No two days are alike around our house." She tried for a normal-looking smile but, not sure she'd achieved it, said, "I've got to talk to someone before class," and hurried into the building.

Jana went directly to her classroom and was one of the three earliest arrivals, as it turned out. Choosing a back corner seat, she opened her text-book to review several points she hoped she remembered correctly from her late-night studies.

She was as relieved as any of the others that there was no quiz but had reason to believe she'd have made out okay had there been one. She passed her homework forward with everyone else's, and Dr. Sally Carlisle gathered the papers at the front of the class, put them all in her leather folder and began her teaching.

The woman must be close to retirement age, and had spent over thirty-five years teaching math courses in this institution. Jana marveled at her still keeping so much enthusiasm for each subject that many students deliberately chose her as their teacher.

And yet, again, Jana was annoyed when she had to several times pull her attention to what was being said.

The class was eventually over, and she joined the many heading for the student union building where they would eat lunch. Jana, however, went on to where the noon meeting was always held.

She slipped into the circle of chairs and was pleased by the number of students who made a point of saying they missed her when she wasn't with them and mentioning they'd been praying for Michael and for her. By the time Todd arrived, Linda was seated on her right and someone else on her left. He took the chair just beyond Linda.

The scripture, prayer and singing went smoothly, and Lizbet did, indeed, have an excellent message about reaching out to others, even to those showing no sign of being ready to receive one's care or love. She gave examples of this from the Bible, from history and from here at the college, and her closing challenge was eloquent.

Jana felt better as she left for her afternoon

class, and told herself she really did need to come more regularly to these sessions. She sometimes did on those two days when she had afternoon labs, but often spent that hour or more in the library; it was quiet there, and being uninterrupted meant she could get more accomplished than was usually possible at home.

On her way to the house in the afternoon, she decided she must tell Gram and Barb about Ray's request that no one know of their being together. She should have done so last night, but had been too hurt and confused to share it with anyone.

And, to be honest, today was not much better!

Jana felt strong enough to do it now, so she walked up the steps, into the house and to the kitchen, greeting Gram. "It smells wonderful here! What is it? Pumpkin pie?"

"Just that and apple today." Gram chuckled. "With the little ones around much of the time, I decided to take advantage of their nap time to do some baking, but didn't want to push the time restraints."

Jana glanced around. "It seems abnormal to not have even one or two of them running through the hall to greet me. Is everyone well and happy?"

"They seem to be—at least well. Michael wasn't happy about going to bed when he did, claiming he wasn't even one teeny, tiny bit sleepy."

"Wouldn't it be great if they could put us to bed instead? We'd appreciate it!" She set her books on the sideboard and went to the refrigerator. "I meant to take an apple or sandwich along for lunch, but forgot to."

Gram didn't look up from rolling out another crust, the final one. "I don't believe you were thinking about lunch then, or at breakfast, either."

"Well, I did have to get ready for school."

"Ah, yes." Gram turned the flattened dough over and glanced at Jana with raised brows as she gave it another several practiced smoothings with her rolling pin. "School."

Jana removed packages of cheese and luncheon meat and the jar of mustard before closing the door. "You're amazing, Gram. With all the early-morning confusion and the girls bringing their little ones, how did you have time to notice that I hardly ate any breakfast?"

"You know I love you, Jana," Gram said, fitting the crust in the pie pan. "Why wouldn't I notice when you're unhappy?"

There was that tightness in Jana's throat again, and she swallowed hard as she brought a knife and luncheon plate along with bread to the end of the table. She sat down and watched Gram's capable hands begin to trim the crust.

"Michael and I did have a wonderful time with Professor Hawkins yesterday…"

Gram continued her pie making but looked at Jana with a smile of encouragement, to which Jana responded by saying, "It was when we were almost home that…" *How can I tell even Gram about this? But I must.* "He asked me to not tell anyone at school about our being together."

That sentence seemed to hang there in the kitchen's stillness, which was broken only by the faint ticking of the wall clock. Gram poured the rest of the pumpkin mixture into the pie shell and sprinkled cinnamon over it before coming to sit beside Jana. "Did he say why?"

She shook her head. "It has to be because of me, because of who I am."

"And just who do you consider yourself to be, Jana?"

"Well, I had Michael with me and no husband

in sight. He probably suspects that I have never been married.''

''You don't think he'd have considered that before? I thought he specifically invited the two of you.''

''He did, but—''

Gram went on as though she hadn't spoken. ''And if he took you to the place he loves so much, and introduced you to all those people at the meeting, and invited you back there and for dinner yesterday, what makes you think he's suddenly ashamed of you or embarrassed by possible opinions of others?''

''But—''

''What was his answer when you asked why he'd said that?''

She squirmed uncomfortably, feeling like the insecure teen she'd been when first coming here. ''I didn't ask.''

''Why was that, dear?'' Gram's flour-dusted hand covered hers on the table. ''Why didn't you ask him?''

''I couldn't. I really couldn't.'' Gram was silent again, and Jana found herself going on even though she didn't want to. ''I couldn't bear to hear him put in words that he didn't approve of my being unmarried and having a three-year-old son. That it looked bad for a professor—'' she emphasized that word ''—to be seen with someone like me.''

There was both sympathy and strength in the look she was receiving from Gram, but Jana wanted encouraging words, and they weren't being given. ''What he said upset me so much that I carried Michael into the house with me and told him to leave the car seat on the porch before he left.''

''So how did you make out in class today? You did go, didn't you?''

''Yes, I went.''

''And?''

''And I tried to avoid looking directly at him, which was difficult to do without being terribly obvious,'' she admitted, attempting a self-deprecating grin.

''So you still don't know what's going on, right?''

''Right. But, Gram,'' Jana said, leaning toward her, ''there's nothing right about this! We'd had such a wonderful time together.''

The buzzer sounded, and Gram got up to take two pies from the upper rack of the oven, move

those from the bottom to the top and replace
those with the final two. In the process of doing
that, she suggested, "Maybe, Jana, you have to
think about this some more."

"That's almost all I've done since last evening," she admitted, "just going over and over
that scene. And the situation doesn't look any
brighter now than it did then."

"No brighter at all?"

"Well, not much. And I certainly didn't enjoy
his class today!"

"He didn't do as good a job as usual?"

"Oh, I suppose he did." She was spreading
mustard over her slice of bread, meticulously
covering every bit of its surface. "He must have,
I suppose. Everyone agrees he's an excellent
teacher, but that doesn't mean that I personally
got as much from it as I should have!"

"Did he seem to be trying to make eye contact?"

"I think so, but I can't say for sure. I didn't
want him thinking I was trying for that with
him."

"Why?"

"I don't want him thinking I'm that giddy, that
desperate for a man that I have no pride at all."

"That old pride thing again."

"Gram!" she protested. "Wouldn't you be hurt if someone told you he didn't want anyone to know he was seeing you?"

"But Ray didn't tell you that, at least not as I'm understanding from what you said. It was only one group, one category of people he didn't want to know right now, which makes me wonder about the why of that situation. Why is it okay for the doctor and the cleaning woman and all those others at the railroad club to know about you, to actually get introduced to you by him, yet those at the college aren't to even hear about it?

"That desire on his part is totally unrealistic, for that matter. A college campus is in some ways like a small town, with everyone interested in everyone else's business."

Jana nodded. "I'll agree with you on that."

There seemed a flicker of humor in Gram's eyes before she said seriously, "But remember that's not always a bad thing. Sometimes what seems unbearable at the time works out for the best."

"I know." She took a bite of her sandwich and took her time chewing and swallowing before asking, "Do you have any idea how annoying that last statement of yours was when I first came here?''

Gram laughed. ''I suspect that, unfortunately, it hasn't got too much less annoying now, four years later.''

Jana pushed back her chair and stood up, leaning over to hug this woman she couldn't love more if they were related by blood. ''I'll have to admit it hasn't, but now it's especially bothersome because I've learned how true it is. And, if I'm to believe that, I should keep a more open mind than I want to.'' She returned to her seat. ''Frankly, it's often more satisfying at the moment to just work up a good mad.''

''It never does get easy, not for anyone,'' Gram said.

''Even you?''

''Even me. I've worked at conquering that bugaboo most of my life and still have times when I have to give myself a strict lecture, then deliberately decide to shape up.''

''That's almost discouraging. Here I've been telling myself it will get easier as I get older, that I'll learn from my experiences and those of others.''

''As to what I've learned from my own many

years of experiences, it's to recognize just a little earlier my weaknesses and wayward thoughts so I can get a quicker start on correcting attitudes and responses."

There was a call from upstairs, and Jana hurried to bring down the first child to awaken, hoping the others, especially Michael, would sleep longer. Candace, an easygoing youngster six weeks older than he, had discovered the joy of colors. She now sat at the kitchen table with a glass of milk, the big box of fat crayons and a tablet, busily creating vaguely recognizable trees, flowers and animals.

She was not as talkative as some of the others, but her enunciation was good, like now, when she stated, "Michael's lucky, he went in a great big black train."

"Yes, he did, Candi. Did he tell you what he did while there?"

"A nice man let him ring the bell. And blow the whistle."

"That's right. He did blow that whistle, real loud."

Candi stopped coloring, even laid down the bright pink crayon she'd been using, and looked up pleadingly. "If I'm real, real good, Aunt Jana, can I go with Michael next time?"

Next time! There will probably never be a next time for any of us, not with Ray. "We'll see, dear," she said, trying to keep her voice light.

"Okeydokey." Looking happy with what she construed as a promise, Candi returned to her activity, covering more of the page with squiggles, scrawls and lines.

Tearing off the sheet, she held it toward Gram. "You want my pretty picture?"

Gram accepted it with admiration. "I certainly do want that, Candi. Did you color it just for me?"

"Mm-hmmmm."

The paper was laid down in front of Candi, and Gram leaned over her. "Tell me all about your picture, dear."

"Wel-l-l, here is the train," she said, pointing to a black line running more or less diagonally from the top left corner, "and here's Michael and me and Aunt Jana. And here and here and here," she said, pointing at a different spot with each word, "are pretty stones and cars and the station and extra railroad tracks and flowers and the 'fessor."

Jana didn't catch that last word until she noticed Gram's amused glance. *Michael has certainly gone into detail as to our activities yesterday, and with whom!*

She felt that twinge of almost loneliness again, and commanded her errant thoughts to leave the professor—Ray? Dr. Hawkins? She didn't even know what to call the man in her thoughts, for goodness sake!

Well, so much for that concern. I'm just going to forget him, except, of course, for his teaching that class I chose to take.

Chapter Nine

Since this was one of the days when Barb got home from school fairly early and was scheduled to look after the little ones, Jana decided to walk with Gram. "Y'know, you're hard on my ego," she complained after about a mile. "Here I am, puffing at your fast pace, and you're just breezing along."

Gram laughed but did go slower. "This is nothing compared with doing that physical therapy following my hip fracture," she stated. "And I don't want to go through that again if I can help it. There's no reason for racing through my several miles, but I got in that habit when I used to think I was really needed at the house or told myself that, anyway."

"You are definitely needed there, and always will be."

"I want to be, so keeping myself in good physical condition seems like the best insurance policy not just as to my bones, heart and lungs, but my mental well-being."

Jana nodded. "It's mostly a lack of self-discipline in my case."

"I don't agree." Gram kept on walking. "You're a remarkably disciplined young woman, successfully juggling your full load of classwork with taking care of the children and doing your share of the housework. And, whether or not you get around to taking an extended walk each day, you do get a lot of exercise."

That was true enough that no comments were necessary, so Jana pointed out the display of spring flowers at the house they were passing.

By the time she got home, Jana was feeling good about this day and looking forward to spending time with her studies. She and Gram went to the kitchen to enjoy the pot of tea Barb had begun steeping when Michael brought the report that Mama and Gram were starting down the block.

All three women were sitting at the table when

Barb said, "By the way, Jana, some of us were talking about you today, the way you spontaneously jumped in to help Todd with that dog-and-cage act the other night."

"I'm not sure *spontaneously* is the right word for that, Barb." Jana laughed, recalling the fun of participating. "I'd certainly had no idea of doing such a thing, but he whispered the request and I went along with it."

"Well, Nicki Livingston, Todd's sister, was in that room at the time. He's apparently tried to get her to help on other occasions, but she never did, so was most impressed when you went along with it so willingly—and well!"

"Actually, Michael stole the show from both of us."

"It would be hard for mere adults to top that," Barb agreed. "But anyhow, Nicki didn't know until today about our living here in the same house, but then she asked how long you'd been dating the professor."

"What? How did you get from the invisible dog to Dr. Hawkins?"

"How do conversations ever get where they do?" Barb shrugged broadly. "Apparently Todd told her he really likes you and was going to ask you out, so when Nicki was at her part-time job as a waitress at the Old Station this weekend and saw you together, she wanted to know if that was serious.''

Jana looked toward Gram and saw the small frown lines between her brows. ''I hope you informed her that it is nothing at all. We'd just been at the same place during the afternoon, then went to dinner together.''

Barb shook her head. ''I didn't word it like that, of course, but said I thought it was just a friendly get-together, that Dr. Hawkins had been concerned about Michael's having been so sick and wanted to take him to see the train.''

''That's perfect!'' *What a relief.* ''Thanks.'' She and Gram were smiling.

It was during the following day's embryology class that Ray felt he had to make several announcements. ''As you may remember, one student from this class dropped out during the first week, which was all well and good, and there's no damage to his record or his credibility as a student.

''Another person came to see me yesterday, planning to do likewise. There is no reason for her or for any of you to remain unless you wish to do so—except that, as I explained to her, there are facts that apparently need elucidating.

"People leaving any class in this institution this far into a course will automatically receive an incomplete, which is made note of in the office of the academic dean. Racking up more than one of these, except for severe physical or other conditions, can be a matter of concern to them, for if a student is really trying and still having difficulty making the grade, they'll try working with him or her, even arranging for tutors to help, if necessary.

"However, if that student is not trying, that, too, will become a matter of record."

And then he added, "And one thing more. Should the course in question be required for a chosen degree, that student will obviously have to repeat and receive a passing grade in it either with the same or a different teacher."

There was a shuffling of feet, and students glanced around, undoubtedly wondering who it was who'd provoked this dissemination of information.

"I want to stress again that this is the position of the institution, and my own personal opinions

have nothing whatsoever to do with any consequences.''

And he went directly into the lesson.

He assumed that Jana would be one of those
trying to determine which student was absent or,
more likely, had considered leaving. They'd
probably never guess it to be Grace Torres, the
tall, tanned, athletic woman who always sat in
the back row and had not asked a question or
contributed anything in class during the entire semester.

While teaching, he couldn't keep from glancing at Grace from time to time, noting that she
was, indeed, taking notes on what he was saying,
but he'd checked his records and knew that she
was below the borderline as to passing and would
need an almost perfect grade on the final exam
to bring it up enough.

Following the class, several students crowded
around him, talking about his opening remarks.
Neither Jana nor Grace was among them.

For the first time since Sunday night, however,
Jana had looked directly into his eyes when he
was finishing that preliminary announcement.
And there might have been a slight smile on her

face when their glances met for an instant as she left.

Those students at the front of the room gave wholehearted support, even if they did keep him from speaking with Jana.

He returned to his office, remembering her being here with him those two times she'd used his phone. Was there any chance she'd ever be back? The only way that could happen was if he talked with her face-to-face and explained the reason behind his request. But even if she should understand, how could he continue arranging times to be with her, knowing that had consequences?

He'd been pleased when given this office, but today was frustrated by there being too little space for pacing. Well, he could use this time to finish preparations for one of his laboratory sessions. He'd gathered books and papers and was starting for the door when there was a knock on it.

A student delivering mail to faculty and other offices was standing there, holding out a bundle of magazines, flyers and two envelopes. "Good morning, Dr. Hawkins."

"Thanks, Bruce." Ray was already glancing at the upper left corner of the top envelope as he automatically told the young man, "Have a good day."

Heading back for his desk, he sat down to slit open both letters, even though suspecting one to be a cleverly crafted advertisement for something he wasn't interested in. It was, and he tossed it in the basket before sliding the single sheet of paper from the unstamped but sealed envelope from the personnel office. He expected it to be another of those frequent little announcements or suggestions for which Henry Capper was notorious, but this one proved to be personal.

"Dear Ray," was scrawled on a sheet of his letterhead paper, instead of the full name and title. "Something recently came to my attention about which I must speak with you as soon as possible. Please call my office when you read this. Thanks, Hank Capper."

I wonder if it's about that Torres woman! Perhaps she's so bent out of shape that she's run over there and raised a stink. Well, Ray was sorry things worked out this way, but at least Henry—*Hank*, as he'd signed—seemed to be a sensible man, and they'd got along well in the past.

He punched in Hank's phone extension, and

the call was answered by a pleasant-voiced woman telling him that Mr. Capper would like Ray to come as soon as possible. "Right away?" he asked.

"That would be appreciated, Dr. Hawkins. I'll tell him to expect you in a few minutes."

Ray didn't feel comfortable about this; Hank's leaving word with his secretary to have him come as soon as his call came through didn't sound good!

He locked his office and strode across the campus to the administration building and into Hank's outer office. "I'm Raymond Hawkins."

"Yes, I know," the attractive middle-aged woman said pleasantly. "Mr. Capper's waiting for you, so go on in."

He opened the door and walked toward the desk, smiling as he commented, "I take it we have a problem?"

Hank didn't return the smile. "There well could be." He was indicating the seat to his right, at the side of the desk, not across it, which seemed like a good sign to Ray.

"What is it?"

Hank rolled his armed chair a little closer. "I hope this is nothing more than a misunderstanding, an assumption on the part of someone, for otherwise you may be in trouble.''

"*Trouble?*"

Hank tilted his head to the side, then moved it up and down just once. "I've just been informed that you are blatantly dating one of your students and that you're giving her grades she doesn't deserve. As you know, that is not acceptable.''

Ray sank back against the straight chair, aware of the pounding of his heart and the sucked-in air that seemed stuck in his chest. *"What?"*

Hank didn't repeat his statement, just asked, "Is that correct?''

He wanted to shout out that it was a lie, for he'd done nothing wrong, nothing immoral, but instead he asked, "Who brought you such an absurd report?''

A shake of Hank's graying head and a slight frown let Ray know that this question wasn't about to be answered, so he stated, "It isn't true, not really. I have been with a young woman and her son a couple of times, but not *dating*. I took flowers—''

He was interrupted by Hank asking, "This young woman is one of your students?''

"Well, yes—but the flowers were for her

three-year-old son, not for her! She'd mentioned in front of the whole class that he was real sick in the hospital, and I thought I'd like to take him something—which turned out to be a ceramic steam engine planter. Filled with plants, obviously.''

"And?"

This is worse than I could have imagined! And I don't know how much to tell. "Well, his mother was there with the little fellow, and so was her grandmother, who suggested that I take Jana down to the hospital's cafeteria, since she'd eaten no lunch. I hadn't, either, so we did go there together, but there was most certainly nothing of a dating nature.''

Hank again nodded once, while asking, "And that was your only time alone together?''

"*Alone?* With people at almost every table in the cafeteria? You've got to be kidding!'' Ray could only hope that taking this tack might help.

It didn't. Henry Capper continued sitting there, hardly moving a muscle, and Ray tried to match that when he said, "Because of that little gift, we started talking about trains. I don't know if you're aware that I have a special interest in them and belong to a railroad club and spend many hours helping restore some of the old equipment there.

"Anyway, it turns out that she likes trains, too, so—well, both of us went to the monthly railroad meeting. But that wasn't a date, either, just two people going to a meeting!"

Again he hoped that would be enough, but found it wasn't when Hank said quietly, "And I suppose you're going to tell me that your taking her and her son out for dinner was not a date, either."

"But it *wasn't,*" he stated, leaning forward in his chair, hand on the large mahogany desk. "At least if by 'date' you're thinking of hugging or kissing or even holding hands—at no time has there been any of that. We are both—all three of us, that is—interested in trains, as I said before, so we went back down to the station on Sunday afternoon, then on to the Old Station Restaurant to eat, so the little boy would have the experience of sitting in a real restored railroad dining car and watching and hearing several long trains go past. And that's all there was to it!"

"You were seen there. And the person reporting that seems to think there was much more going on than that."

"That person is lying if she—or he—says we did anything wrong. We did not. Neither there nor elsewhere."

"Still no 'hugging or kissing or holding hands'?"

He recognized the repetition of his own words. "That is correct. None of those things, not a single one of them."

They talked about the matter for the next quarter-hour, and Ray came to the conclusion that the person making this report was deliberately attempting to get him in trouble. Was there any possibility there might be consequences as far as the college was concerned? He finally asked, "How many people know about this accusation and about our talking here today?"

"Not many yet, though I must warn you that it looks like you have an enemy. If something's not done about this matter in the near future, word of it will undoubtedly spread in a fashion that can harm not only you, but us."

Ray returned to his office, took off his suit jacket and noted that his shirt was damp. *You might tell others you're not scared, Raymond Hawkins. You just told Hank that. But you are and have every reason to be.*

*You're not even sure who this enemy is! It
could be someone other than that Torres woman,
and for another reason. Even that other student
I gave a zero to last week in addition to Grace,
when they turned in reports that were exactly the
same. I was so sure the report was plagiarized
by both of them that I went online looking for it,
then included copies of the original along with
the returned papers.*

*Maybe I shouldn't have mentioned that in
class, but I didn't give their names when stating
that such a practice would not be tolerated, that
any papers I found to be stolen or written by
someone other than the student would automatically receive a zero. And if he or she cheated
once, I'd be watching like a hawk to make sure
it didn't happen again.*

He was grateful for the three-hour laboratory
session that afternoon. He walked around making
sure everyone knew what was to be done, and
how, but also what the purpose of it was and
what they were learning from it.

He was so occupied that he had little time for
fretting and worrying, although the matter still
remained in the back of his mind.

From the very first, his lab sessions had the

requirement of each person leaving his area immaculate, and today was no exception. One woman and a man needed reminding, and stayed long enough to make everything clean and neat.

As far as he could tell, there was no antagonism or hatred from anyone in this class, but how could he know for sure?

He returned to the office long enough to leave his lab coat and pick up his suit coat and the two magazines that had come in today's mail. He told himself he couldn't face checking over test results tonight, so left the day's exams in a locked desk drawer.

Home—it felt like a sanctuary, and he gradually regained some of that sense of peace he usually found here, though not as much as he'd hoped for.

Who had gone out of her or his way to try to get him in trouble? What was the motive? Where had he and Jana been other than that restaurant? How long had the perpetrator been looking for a way to get even for whatever caused such antagonism? Why was the individual doing this?

Several times he'd considered the possibility of picking up the phone and talking to Jana, but he wasn't at all sure she'd accept his call. And he also wasn't sure if he could handle that kind of rejection tonight.

It was after nine-thirty when he convinced himself to try.

Michael had been in bed for an hour or two, and Jana had finished studying for the night and was stacking on the sideboard the books and notebooks she would need tomorrow. "At least I have only one course this semester that requires writing a final paper," she told Gram, who'd come to the kitchen for a glass of water.

"And you seem to be enjoying all of them."

"Each semester is more interesting, and—"

The phone rang, and she picked it up, then almost wished Gram had done so when hearing Ray's voice on the other end of the line greeting, "Good evening, Jana. It's good to hear your voice."

"A good evening to you, as well." She was too uncertain to say more than that.

"I have to make an apology, at least an explanation."

"You don't have to, Professor Hawkins."

"Yes, I do. I wanted to explain before I left, but wasn't able to."

Before she'd figured how to word her own apology, or if she even wanted to, he continued, "I now realize that the way my request was worded made it sound inconsiderate, but I didn't mean it the way you apparently took it."

He hesitated again before going on, "Look, Jana, would it be okay for me to come over there tonight? Right away? I'd appreciate speaking with you face-to-face, if possible."

She realized even as she glanced at the wall clock that this was a purely automatic response to the mention of time; no matter what hour it was, she, too, needed to have this straightened out. "All right. I'll be waiting for you on the front porch."

She heard what sounded like an extended exhalation and thought it might be a sigh of relief when he said, "I do appreciate this, Jana, and will be there in just a few minutes."

She gently replaced the phone and continued holding on to it as though it were a link to the man to whom she'd just been speaking.

She went to the downstairs lavatory to run a comb through her hair before going to the front room. Gram had gone there as soon as it was obvious the call wasn't for her, so Jana reported Ray's expected arrival.

"Good!" Gram started to rise from the blue recliner. "And this seems like a good time for me to wish you a good night and happy dreams."

Jana shook her head. "You don't have to do that, Gram. For that matter, it may be helpful to have someone with your stability in our general area."

"Oh, I'm sure you'll do fine." Smiling encouragement and love, Gram walked up the steps to her room, and Jana went out on the porch.

Chapter Ten

This April evening was balmy, more like the beginning of June, and Jana was comfortable in the short-sleeved blouse and summer-weight jeans she'd worn to school. She started to sit in one of the old, green-painted rockers, then deliberately chose the equally old and similarly painted two-person swing.

I wonder how many members of how many generations have sat on this swing as children, shared secrets as adolescents, hugged and kissed as lovers, nursed babies and sung lullabies and played with their children, then slowly moved back and forth, back and forth, whiling away the hours when they grew old.

She was smiling as she saw the dark car pull up to the curb, heard the smooth-running motor silenced, then watched as the door opened and the interior light came on, revealing the man she'd been waiting for. She was pleased that the people who'd been sitting on their porch next door had recently gone inside, and she hadn't noticed anybody on the porch behind her.

She walked across to meet him as he came rapidly up the walk and started up the steps, but neither of them said anything until he was standing on the last step, right in front of her, their eyes on a level. "Thanks, Jana, for permitting me to come."

"I'd been afraid you never would again."

He reached for her hand, which she extended toward him, and he walked with her back to the swing, not speaking until they were seated. "I was afraid you might be too angry to let me do so."

How open, how honest can I be with him? "It wasn't anger that made me turn away," she said softly. "It was hurt. I thought you were ashamed of me, that—"

"Ashamed of you?" He was staring at her as though with disbelief. "I can't conceive of ever being ashamed of you, Jana. Everything I know of you fills me with admiration, and I loved introducing you to my friends and acquaintances!''

"But you—"

"Those in my railroad group welcomed you with no question. They like you, and so do I!''

"Then, why did you say what you did about not letting people know about us?''

"I was almost sure that was what bothered you, and I'm especially sorry about that, for my regard for you had nothing to do with the way I worded that.'' He shoved his spread fingers through his medium-length hair. "It's just that our college has had an especially tight sexual harassment policy these last years.

"There have been several situations—one just before I came. A well-thought-of professor in the music department overstepped all bounds of propriety by playing favorites, exchanging good marks for specific responses and withholding good marks from others who didn't go along with his desires.

"Everyone knew about it by the time he was forced to leave. It was on the news and in the papers, and he was threatening to sue for defamation of character. It was one big, horrific mess!"

"That must have been before I came," she admitted.

His lips were set in a straight line as he nodded. "The lawyers for the college worked overtime, and it was only when a couple of the women he'd used agreed to go to court on a sexual harassment charge that he finally voluntarily left.

"The legalities of all that gave our institution a whole new awareness of its vulnerability, as well as that of the individual students, so, since then, they've kept a sharp eye out for anything they consider suspicious."

"Well," she said, relaxing against the swing, "at least we've done nothing anyone could be suspicious of." There was such a long silence that she looked toward him and saw how uncomfortable he appeared.

"I was called into the office of the personnel director today, Jana."

Their swinging came to an abrupt stop. "Whatever for?"

"Somebody went to a member of the board and also to the college president about our 'dating,' our 'being together all the time.' Either the same individual or someone else did the same in personnel.''

"But we've done nothing at all to warrant accusations!''

"I told him that and I think he believes me, but not everyone will.''

She sank back against the swing again. "Yes, many will believe the accuser, especially with what they'll undoubtedly consider my unsavory past—my precious, innocent little son.''

His arm came around her shoulders, but she didn't permit herself to lean into the comfort of his embrace even when he said, "I've come to like Michael very much.''

"I appreciate that, and your kindness in including him when we went to see the train. And for dinner.''

"It was not kindness, nor generosity, nor anything like that. You have a fine, loving, very intelligent little boy, and I not only enjoy his company, but would be proud to introduce him, too, to any friend or colleague!''

"Thanks.'' She turned to look into his face. "I admit to being too often defensive. For that matter, Gram keeps reminding me of that. Perhaps I should tell you why, what led to my pregnancy."

"No."

Hardly able to believe he'd said that, she repeated his single word. "No?"

"It's not that I don't want to know all about you, even your history and background, for I do, but not tonight, not when you'd be giving it because you think you owe me since I was called on the carpet today.

"Sometime when we're both ready to do so for the right reasons, then I'd be honored to learn everything you're willing to share with me."

"Thank you." It was only a whisper, all she could manage right then.

Ray heard those words, so softly spoken by those lovely lips that seemed to be somewhat tremulous, and his heart ached for whatever pain was in hers. He longed to reach out to her, to give the comfort of his arms, to hold her close. *As I would with Michael, if her little boy needed it.*

But then he realized how inaccurate, how incomplete that thought had been, and was almost shocked by the realization that he'd already come to love Michael, and that his love for the child's mother included a different, much stronger kind, as well.

That was such a surprise that he broke the rhythm of their sitting there quietly, swinging back and forth. "I would like to kiss you, Jana." *How long has it been since I said that to a girl? Perhaps when I was twelve?*

"I'd like that, too," she murmured, but raised her hand to cup his cheek. "I think, though, it's best not to do that, either. You could be called up in front of the president, or the board, I suppose, and it may be important to be able to honestly repeat to them that we have never kissed.

"And I was just thinking about what you told personnel about our never hugging. Does your arm around my shoulder count as that?"

"Not to me, it doesn't! I want to enfold you within my arms and press you close to my heart—that's what I call a hug." His little laugh was rueful. "And perhaps you should know that I'm making a real effort to remain true to what I said today."

They spoke about school and the town, of Gram and her many activities and of members of her family, especially Vanessa and her husband, whom Ray knew at least by sight because of attending three funerals at the mortuary he co-owned.

Their companionship on the porch this pleasant evening was so manifest that Jana did mention some things concerning her past—about coming here almost four years ago, about the same time as Barb and three other pregnant girls did, in order to have their babies.

"So your class, your teaching is especially meaningful for me—reinforcing again what I kept insisting to my parents, what made me leave home rather than have the abortion they insisted upon."

"You don't need my feeble words," he stated. "Every time you look at your son, every time you pick him up and hold him, you're reminded of the certainty of that truth."

"You understand?"

"Yes. I understand."

I'm grateful you're leaving this soon. She tried to convince herself of that as she watched him drive away, and one part of Jana—her sane self, she scoffed—really meant it. But the very human part of her was hungry for his kisses, his holding her and speaking romantic words.

She'd had all of those for a very short time with Jerry Brighton. He'd been good at all of them! He was blessed with a spontaneous, happy demeanor which everyone enjoyed, and she'd happily grown up with him, in a manner of speaking, although he was three years older. Their parents were good friends and often played golf together at the country club, and she and Jerry were frequently with them for golf or skiing or horseback riding, especially when they shared vacations.

It was at Myrtle Beach that the relationship between the teens changed drastically. Their parents were off somewhere, and he'd come into her hotel room. He reminded her again that he'd be leaving for Princeton in a few days, and she told him she'd be lonely for him and she would miss him a lot!

That's when he put his arms around her—oh, he'd done that before, playfully, and that time when she was hurt while skiing the winter before—but not like this. He said he'd miss her, too, and that he'd come to love her. And then he began kissing her.

She did try to stop him, sort of, in words, anyway. And even though she enjoyed his touch, she told him she didn't want to get pregnant, but he kept saying how much he loved her and how much he wanted her, and she certainly didn't have to worry about getting pregnant, for he'd been hoping for this, and had "protection" with him.

Only afterward did she realize what a fool she'd been not to wonder how he happened to have that so-called protection with him, and why she'd given in, especially as easily as she had.

She soon learned that the "protection" hadn't prevented her from becoming pregnant.

How quickly Jerry's telling her that he loved her and wanted her did a complete turnabout! He and his parents were the most adamant, even more than her parents, in insisting, demanding, that she have an abortion.

She'd been forbidden to talk with anyone about the situation she was in, but she'd finally been desperate enough to call Grandma Dewise's pastor for an appointment. He'd seen her right away and had cared enough to make the arrangements for her to come to Sylvan Falls.

So it was Gram and her family and friends who had become Jana's family.

When she went upstairs to get ready for bed,

she kissed her sleeping child and, kneeling by his bed, again thanked God for helping her keep her loving, happy, wonderful Michael, the center of her world, the major focus of her love.

Ray did not get called into Personnel or before the president or board, as he'd half expected, but the possibility of its happening was always there, a sword over his head. Common sense told him he should play it safe and not see Jana, but he'd never had such strong feelings for anyone before, and couldn't force himself not to see her.

He showed up for church on Sunday, sitting two rows behind Jana and Gram because he wasn't sure it was expedient for him to sit with them. And he stayed for Sunday school, in Karlyn's class, and was surprised to find that he enjoyed the give-and-take between the members and even the study of the Scriptures.

He came to Gram's for dinner a number of times, and was invited by Karlyn to family activities and to class ones. He and Jana read and reread the college policies concerning sexual harassment, and there was nothing in the words themselves that stated he couldn't date his student, but the folly of doing so was made clear.

For one thing, her being an A student might make it all the more possible for someone out there to say she'd got that in his class for the wrong reasons.

"I suppose I could just not turn in a paper or deliberately not do my best," she'd suggested one day, but the personal integrity of each of them forbade that.

"Would it help if I keep all of my papers, and you keep a record of my responses in class?" she asked, and they decided to do that, even though such an artificial backup could possibly be suspect in itself. For no one else had he been doing that.

"I really do need to maintain high grades, you know," she reminded him one Sunday noon while they were all eating dinner around Gram's table. "Keeping my scholarship is dependent upon my having a good GPA."

"I guess then you'll just have to marry me," Ray said, smiling. "The spouse of a faculty member is automatically given free tuition, if desired."

There was complete silence for a moment as Jana's fork returned to her plate with pie still on it. She stared at him as though wondering if this was a joke, and evidently Gram and Barb must also have been unsure as to what to say or do. Michael, however, pushed his dessert plate to his left, asking, "More cherry pie, Gram?"

That broke the ice, and Gram approved, "Of course you may, dear. You only had a little piece before."

Barb, sitting back in her chair, exclaimed, "Wow, that was the first time in my life that I've heard an actual proposal!"

And Jana was asking Ray at the same time, "You're not serious, are you?"

"I surprised myself as much as I apparently did the rest of you," he admitted, looking around. "I've been thinking about this for some time, and, well, my only apology is to you, Jana. You do know that I love you very much, and you had every right to expect my proposal not to be so public." He reached for her hand. "I hope, I very much hope that its popping out this way doesn't make you think I'm insincere."

She was shaking her head, but that was probably about the last part of what he said. "I know you wouldn't say that insincerely, but don't you think we need to talk about this, just the two of us?"

His hand squeezed hers. "Of course."

Jana didn't look at the other adults at the table. Michael was busy eating his pie, and she reached to blot away the red juice starting down his chin before saying, "Excuse me." Removing her hand from Ray's, she fled to the front room.

I'm completely out of control! she told herself. *Why am I crying? I've loved him for a long time, and he's just asked me to marry him and here I am crying.*

Ray came to where she was sitting on the couch, seated himself beside her and put his arm around her. "I'm sorry I handled things so poorly, Jana. I do realize this wasn't the time and place to say that, and I wouldn't deliberately hurt you for the world."

"It's all right. You did nothing wrong, it's just that..." She accepted from him the tissues he'd removed from the box on the stand and impatiently scrubbed tears from her cheeks. "I promised myself that, before we'd become seriously involved—in case you ever wanted to be—that I'd tell you all about how I happened to become a mother. And I didn't." It was almost a wail.

"You don't have to." His voice was soothing

as he tried to draw her into his embrace. "That was in the past, and I love the woman you are now and the mother you are to Michael."

Even that didn't satisfy her, and she stated doggedly, "And I love you, too, so very much! But you've got to know, Ray. If we should marry..."

"When we marry."

That earned him the hint of a smile, which disappeared immediately. "...It would be forever, and I couldn't stand secrets from the past, or in the future, to come between us.

"Don't you realize there would be times when you'd wonder, when you'd fancy in your mind what took place?"

"I don't think I will, but if I ever should, don't you think our love would be strong enough for me to ask such a question then, and for you to answer?"

"I'd hope so, but I couldn't bear to have you reject me, not then, not when we'd become one, not when we might even have children."

He tried to convince her of his faithfulness, but eventually he must have realized that, since her parents, those she'd trusted all her life, had found it far too easy to turn their backs on her, she had no basis for trusting him.

Apparently against his better judgment, he finally said he'd listen, but only if she'd promise to remember, forever, that she'd been the one to insist on this.

And when she'd finished, so afraid this would make him turn away from her, he was finally able to prove to her that, if such a thing were possible, he loved her even more.

"Perhaps you've been right in being so insistent," he told her, "but it wasn't necessary. No matter what, I want to be married to you soon, you beautiful, courageous, unbelievably strong and loving woman. You have given up so much to be true to what you were convinced was right."

The semester seemed to be going unusually slowly for Ray, undoubtedly because he and Jana had decided to be as circumspect as possible while yet spending as much time as they could with one another at Gram's or far enough away from the campus that they weren't apt to be seen.

But they soon wondered how far they had to go, for they ran into several of her classmates while visiting Corning Glass in New York state. Gram and Barb were with the three of them, and Gram also accompanied them to Steamtown, where a colleague of Ray's from the history department stopped to talk.

On both occasions, Gram did much of the visiting even though she'd not known the others. Because of her friendly demeanor and inclusiveness, Ray and Jana told themselves there wasn't too much probability of tales being deliberately spread.

Jana picked up extra brochures at both places and, when writing her weekly missives to her parents, included one of these at two different times. She also occasionally put in a picture of Michael, or of Michael and herself, especially when these showed them with trains or anything having to do with railroads.

She'd still received no reply nor acknowledgment from them, and Ray asked, "How long are you going to continue putting yourself through this?"

He half expected her to be defensive, but she wasn't. "I'm just leaving the door open, Ray," she told him. "They may never walk through it, but they—or even one of them—just might.

"I'm not ruling out that God can arrange even that, and I like to think that Michael may some day have grandparents."

He loved being with her, just the two of them or with others. She was well-read, intelligent and an excellent conversationalist, and he couldn't envision having a boring moment with her. He also respected and admired her willingness to discuss anything, everything with him.

He tried to be that open with her, except for one confession he never intended to make, convinced as he was that he wasn't really a jealous man. It was just that Todd was often waiting for Jana in the hall or arranging to walk out of the classroom with her or trying to get her to commit to coming to that noon meeting he was so involved with!

Ray had been away for several days at a seminar and didn't expect to return until very late Sunday night. However, deciding to forgo the evening session, he checked out of the hotel in the morning and left as soon as the noon meal and speech were over.

He was starting down Gram's block when he saw Todd slam the door of his car and hurry up the walk toward the porch. The sight was like a punch in the stomach to Ray, for he'd so looked forward to surprising Jana and being with her.

Todd didn't look around, just opened the door and went inside, and Ray could only hope that no one within that house had seen him drive by. *Now what?* he asked himself. *It's hard to believe that the woman I love is seeing Todd behind my back, yet what other reason is there for that young man's being here?*

He drove all the way home before deciding there could be some other explanation for what he'd seen. Either way, he had to know the truth. Without getting out of his car, he drove around the circular driveway and started back.

Then he saw Jana and Michael at the edge of town, coming out of McDonald's with ice-cream cones! He was greeted with so much welcome and enthusiasm by both of them that Ray told them he hadn't eaten anything, so if they'd wait until he bought a chocolate cone, too, they'd all ride back together.

It was on the way there that Jana, without having any idea of what a fool he was, mentioned that Todd was expected this evening. It was the second time Barb was going out with him, the first date having been set up by his sister, a class-mate of hers.

Ray didn't admit what a relief this was, not only because he'd fretted about Todd's being a possible rival for Jana's affections, but also that the younger man might have been the talebearer to the college. After all, it was his sister who'd seen Jana and Michael with Ray at that restaurant just before he'd been called on the carpet.

And again he promised himself he was going to stop trying to figure out who had tried to make trouble—he didn't want to know.

It was getting near the end of the semester, and he was preparing final examinations for all his classes. He started to mention something about one of these when Jana clapped her hands over both ears. "Don't tell me anything about them, Ray!"

"This isn't one you'll be taking," he assured her. "You know I wouldn't do that, even for you."

She nodded, indicating her awareness of his integrity, but said, "For your sake, though, we can't afford my knowing anything about any of them."

That was another of his life's frustrations. "I'll

be so glad to get married so we no longer have that specter of possible interrogation hanging over us!''

"Oh?'' She was trying to look serious, but he recognized the mischief in her eyes as she added, "So that's why you look forward to being married to me.''

"Not exactly.'' He laughed, too, and, having just parked, kissed her without looking around to see if anyone was watching. "This is but a hint of all I'm looking forward to.''

Exams were over and the grades finally available, with Barb's one B being the only thing keeping both of them from getting straight A's once again. "Ah, well,'' she murmured as they were all together in the kitchen, "I'll keep my scholarship, which is the most important thing.'' She still had one more year before completing the newly available four-year baccalaureate degree in food services.

And that reminded Jana to ask, "When should I go to the financial aid office to release mine, Ray?''

"We have to wait until after we're married in order for you to be qualified for the spousal scholarship, but that will still leave plenty of time for them to give your present one to the next deserving applicant on the list.''

''And that's only two weeks away! Can you believe it?''

Ray laughed. ''I, too, am having difficulty in realizing how fast the weeks are flying by.''

''Do you suppose couples who plan huge weddings with all the pomp and ceremony and a dozen attendants feel like this, too?'' But she repeated something she'd said before. ''I'm so grateful it was okay with you for our marriage to be kept simple.''

Gram joined the conversation and said, ''We've all seen too many that got out of hand socially, financially and emotionally. From what I've observed, I'd guess that more of those end in divorce than the simpler ones.''

They'd agreed that the wedding would immediately follow Sunday morning's service, then right after that there'd be a walk-around luncheon, as Gram called it, in the Family Activity Center. It would be something like the college's open house, but with people moving between tables for their choices of everything from appetizers to meats, vegetables, casseroles and desserts.

And the last table would, of course, feature the bridal cake, which Barb was decorating.

No formal invitations were being sent, but everyone who wished to come would be welcome. Barb had stated from the beginning that she'd like to be in charge of refreshments, and Gram was involved, too, even though a half dozen of Barb's classmates were pitching in.

Jana had not chosen this style because it was different or because it was simpler, but because she wanted it this way, and she appreciated and loved even more this man she was marrying, because he didn't try to talk her out of it.

Chapter Eleven

It was nine days later that Ray received his second missive from Henry Capper, with a request similar to the previous one, and this time Hank didn't seem as cordial. "I understand you're still seeing Miss Jenson."

He couldn't keep from smiling, even though Henry's statement lacked warmth. "And I'll be seeing much more of her in less than a week."

"Oh?"

Ray laughed aloud as he reached out in the timeless tradition of inviting someone to shake hands. The seated man offered his hand but obviously didn't expect it to be retained for the time it took to say, "You're invited, too, if you'd care to come. It's at the end of the ten-thirty service this coming Sunday morning.''

"For what?''

"For our wedding.''

He was still smiling when Hank motioned him to a seat, saying, "You do believe in complicating your life, don't you, Ray?''

"Well, some have told me that marriage does that to them.'' He deliberately refused to take offense at the other man's manner. "However, I'm personally looking forward to it, whether it's complicated or not.''

"We do have a problem.''

"This is beginning to sound like an old record. What is it this time?''

"The same old thing, Ray, and it sounds as though I should have got back with you long before this.''

Ray waited, but when Hank said nothing to fill the next few seconds, he asked, "The same person or persons?''

"It seems to be, only the woman in on it now claims she was unfairly given an F on both her term paper and as her final mark, and it's because she wouldn't give you what you wanted sexually.''

I must keep calm, find out what's going on. "Which of my classes is she in?"

"I'm not sure," Hank admitted. "But she claims you gave your sweetie pie A's on both her paper and test."

"Jana's in only one of my classes, embryology, and I assure you she deserved those marks. I'm fairly sure she'd keep the term paper, after working so hard on it, and also the returned test, so you can see for yourself.

"As for the other woman, several flunked the final, but only two students received failing grades on their papers, Bill Matthewson and Grace Torres. I discovered they'd plagiarized their term papers from an article I found on the Internet!"

"Can you prove that?"

"I can. This was an important assignment, and they were told at the beginning of the semester that twenty percent of their final mark would be based on their research paper. I rarely photocopy class work before passing it back, but did for several really excellent ones, and one of those was Jana's. And, incidentally, I personally asked each of these students if I might keep the copy in my files.

"But I also copied those of Miss Torres and Mr. Matthewson, just in case they might be tempted to contest their scores. And I made a copy of the article I found on the Internet.

"So, yes, those zeros do mean that neither student, who might otherwise have squeaked by with a C minus or a D, passed my course."

They discussed the matter for some time before Ray went to his office and made duplicates for Hank of the article and of the research papers submitted by the students.

Ray was still somewhat worried about the meeting as he walked across the campus to his office after delivering these, but tried to hold on to the fact that Hank had the reputation for fighting for what was right, whether for or against a teacher, so he'd probably handle this well.

Ray had told Hank about their arrangements as to getting married in just four more days, and Hank smiled and gave his best wishes and congratulations. But then he said, "Don't be too surprised if they try to make a case about your marrying her in order that she can't be forced to testify against you. But we'll hope not."

"I certainly do hope not! We'd obviously been

planning our wedding before learning of their intentions.''

Ray decided to say nothing about that day's meeting, and Jana, Gram and all the rest were so excited about getting things ready for Sunday they didn't seem to notice if he might not be as upbeat as usual.

With the term ended and those responsibilities completed, he spent more time in his apartment, although there seemed little to be done there. When he'd first moved in, he considered having someone come to clean each week or two but, not getting around to that right away, discovered he didn't mind at all keeping this marvelous apartment straightened and ready for guests.

After all, how much dirt and clutter could one person actually make? And as to running the sweeper and dusting and keeping things in order, well, there were always odd minutes or blocks of time when those things got taken care of.

What will it be like having Jana and Michael living here with me? He'd not enjoyed roommates at college, for in both his freshman and sophomore years it had been a matter of two people with widely varied tastes in everything from music to best friends forced to share for uncountable hours the space of one not very large room.

Here, however, there was lots of space, even more than Gram's first floor, though laid out differently. And that reminded him to be sure to ask Jana about a big toy chest for her—for *their* son. The ones at Gram's, into which all toys went before bedtime, were communal, as far as he knew, so perhaps Michael would like to help choose his own.

And he supposed he should be moving, out of child's range, some of the souvenirs and knick-knacks that had meaning to him, even if to no one else. But he didn't get around to doing that as he meandered through the high-ceilinged rooms that had so quickly become home.

He hoped it would be that way for Jana, too. She'd seemed pleased with everything, and said she was looking forward to sharing the place with him, but would she have told him if she didn't like it?

Probably not, he decided. She usually had the right words to use in every situation, and he sensed that the many adjustments she'd already been forced to make in her life caused her to especially appreciate harmony and peace.

Please, God, help me to contribute to that harmony and peace in her life. Help me to be strong yet flexible, wise but not know-it-all, and loving under all circumstances. The dear girl's been hurt too many times already.

He'd gone to the kitchen and was pouring a glass of orange juice before it occurred to him that what he'd just been thinking was a prayer. It had seemed so natural and had come so easily that it was sort of like the prayers around the table at Gram's.

Hey, thanks, God. I appreciate this.

He remembered her pastor—their pastor—Sam Harriman mentioning during one of their pre-marriage sessions the dangers of "being unequally yoked together." Ray had informed the middle-aged man that he'd been baptized as an infant and went through all the catechism and had been confirmed in his early teens, and yes, he'd gladly have his membership transferred to this church.

Ray had then closed his mind to anything more than membership, but he'd just prayed twice, if he counted the thanks. And he'd been enjoying his time with Jana in church, partly because of the good sermons but even more because of the fellowship, learning and fun in Karlyn's class.

Am I changing? Growing?

He felt it coming, then laughed aloud in his solitary apartment. *Yes, my darling Jana, I may not tell you until after we're married, but you've already made many changes in my life and outlook. I can hardly wait to find out all the other ones you probably don't realize you have in store for this man who once thought he preferred being a loner, who thought he'd probably never marry.*

He continued smiling as he remembered thinking kids were such a bother that if he should ever marry, he'd probably ask that they have no children—and here he was about to be married and looking forward to adopting Michael and being his father. And perhaps some day he'd be fathering other children, as well.

They'd explained to Michael about the three of them living together here, and he was excited and happy at that prospect. The adults had fretted that he might be lonely without the other children and Gram, but the fact that he'd been the only child there at night would undoubtedly make that transition easier.

Thinking of his soon-to-be family and father-

ing reminded him of his own parents who, when
he'd called to tell them about getting married,
had said they'd definitely be here for the occasion. Ray asked that they come at least a few
days ahead of time, to get to know their soon-to-
be daughter and grandson, and they seemed to
think this an excellent plan. They'd get back to
him concerning arrangements.

However, the one call he received a little later
that evening proved to be of monumental impor-
tance. Hank Capper had taken it upon himself to
personally show each member of the committee
the proof needed to clear Ray of the untrue accusations against him. Ray was unequivocally
exonerated of unfairly flunking those two students, and the committee members wished Hank
to tell him they wished him happiness as a married man.

His parents did not arrive on his doorstep until
late on Friday afternoon, having already been to
their motel and unloaded the car. They'd been
here only once before, shortly after he'd moved
in, and Mother exclaimed again about the beauty
of the location, the big old house and this apartment.

He'd offered to have them stay here, but

Mother said they didn't want to be in the way, which he stated to be an impossibility. He'd love to make it available to them. After all, there was that extra bedroom—until Michael came.

When Ray called, Jana was delighted to learn they'd got here, and Gram came on the phone to insist on his bringing them along for supper. "But be sure to warn them it's just pot roast, salad and pie. And, oh, yes, Kate and Debbie are here, too."

His parents at first demurred, saying they didn't want to be a bother and would just go to a restaurant, but finally agreed on condition that Gram promise to "not go to any extra fuss for us."

Jana then came on the phone to ask Ray, "Did you have the opportunity of checking on your parents' preference as to how we introduce them to Michael?"

"Uh-oh, I forgot that in the excitement of their having just arrived."

"Well, you can find out and be the one to take care of that here."

"I'd love to."

Jana waited with Michael on the porch swing, but he wanted down immediately when Ray's car pulled to the curb. She walked down the steps with her son, but let him scuttle ahead and into the arms of the tall, beaming man who in less than forty-eight hours would become his father.

Ray's mother, Amanda, a tall, attractive woman looking no more than in her early fifties, had given a big smile and called, "Hello, Jana," but then directed her full attention toward the delighted, bouncing little boy in her son's arms, who was being told that this was Grandma, and that was Grandpa.

He was quite willing to smile and to repeat those words, but wrapped his arms around Ray's neck when this grandpa stranger, a little shorter and stockier than his son, reached out for him. Ray was the one to reassure them that Michael was friendly and outgoing, and to ask that they give him a little time to get to know them.

Jana had reached them by this time, and held out her hand, but was pulled into a bear hug and given a kiss by Ray's father, who stated, "I presume our son has shown you that in the Hawkins family this is how we greet those we love."

Jana laughed, too, and wasn't surprised when Ray's mother also kissed her. "I like this tradition," she told them, and they small-talked their way up the walk and steps to be welcomed by Gram, then led through the hallway to the kitchen, the heart of this home.

It was obvious that Ray had explained the situation about Gram's "girls," for Ray's mother started talking with Debbie's mother right away about her working toward becoming an elementary-school teacher.

The meat and vegetables were served within minutes, along with warm rolls, a Waldorf salad and raw vegetables. As they sat around the table, the conversation touched upon many topics, the one getting the most input, of course, being the upcoming wedding. Amanda asked, "Is that customary in this part of the country—having the wedding at the close of a Sunday morning service?"

Jana welcomed the opportunity to explain. "I considered myself a Christian before coming here, but had not actively participated in worship or fellowship for years. However, this has now become important to me and to Ray.

"We discussed many options and came down to the choice between two of them—either having a worship service as part of our wedding or the wedding as part of a service.'' She looked from Amanda to Raymond, then toward Ray, before saying, ''And you know our decision.''

''I like the idea, and we're both looking forward to being present for it.''

''It will be fairly traditional but not especially fancy or anything,'' Jana said when the subject came up again later, and was again reassured that her future in-laws were sure they'd like whatever was planned.

It was shortly thereafter that, admitting they were exhausted from their two days of driving from Wisconsin to central Pennsylvania, they asked Ray to take them to his place so they could pick up their car and go to the motel.

Ray had looked forward to the arrival of his sister, also, and it seemed like old times when the somewhat beat-up red SUV pulled into the driveway and she bailed out before it came to a full stop. ''Tersh!'' Denise shouted, running to throw her arms around him. ''It's so good to be with you again.''

''Agreed, little sister! It's been much too long a time, especially when you're just out in Pittsburgh, only four or five hours away!'' He reached around her to shake hands with his brother-in-law. "Welcome, George. Did you have a good trip?"

"Yes, we did."

They brought their luggage into Michael's room, as Ray already thought of it, then got freshened up and changed their clothes. Denise came out in a summery blue dress the color of her eyes and twirled in front of Ray, making the skirt flare even more than her below-shoulder-length, almost straight brown hair. "Am I presentable?"

"I've never seen you when you weren't. You look great, Deni."

"Mom insisted this was to be informal, not a typical rehearsal dinner."

"For the excellent reason that there will not be a rehearsal," he agreed. "Tomorrow's service, too, will be informal."

"Y'know, Tersh, I like what I've heard about your Jana. She sounds like my kind of person, a real person."

"She is!"

"Well, you've waited long enough to find her."

"So you've told me during these last several

years. And now that I've found her, there's no way I'd give her time to change her mind.''

"Thus the whirlwind courtship?" George asked.

He readily agreed. ''Thus the whirlwind court-ship!''

Ray drove them to Gram's, and Jana came to greet them. ''We're very grateful you can be with us for the wedding.''

''We wouldn't dream of missing Tersh's wedding,'' Denise stated, then seeing Michael coming down the steps in blue shorts and socks and white shirt and shoes, she began walking toward him, speaking as she came. ''Hi, Michael, I'm Ray's sister, Denise, your aunt Denise, and I've been waiting very impatiently to meet you.''

''I was waitin' to see you, too.'' He reached up his little right hand. ''Mama said you were comin'.''

Denise squatted in front of him, her skirt a puddle of blue on the cement as she tried to be more his size. ''And did you know that boys like you and the aunts of those boys can be good buddies?''

He cocked his head to the side and looked her

up and down before nodding sagely. "Yep, you can be my buddy."

A slow, sweet smile gradually covered her face, and she again reached for his hand. "I am honored to be your buddy, Michael."

"Wanna see my toys?" he asked, turning toward the house.

"I'd like that very much." She stood up and took his hand as they started up the porch steps.

Ray stood there shaking his head. "I'd almost forgotten that about her. No matter how many other people were in the room or general area, within minutes every kid in the place was crowded around her."

"That is the one big disappointment in her life." George sighed. "She was hoping to start a family immediately, and doctors have told us there's no apparent reason we haven't during these six years. She's begun talking about having fertility treatments, if necessary."

Jana's hand slid into Ray's and held on tight, and he returned the grip, his thumb rubbing again and again across the back of her hand. It hardly seemed fair that she had gotten pregnant with one indiscretion and Denise had been unable to do so after trying for years.

There must still be some of that pain there but, Ray thought, *Thanks, God, for Michael, and also for Jana's being so loving, not just toward him but to me and others.*

Ray and Jana were the last to go up the steps, and she asked, "What does your sister call you?"

He laughed. "I should have warned you. As you know, I'm Raymond John Hawkins, the Third, which was usually okay, since they just called me 'Ray.' However, Denise came across the word tertiary, meaning third and, being a year and a half younger than I and resenting what she regarded as my superior attitude, started calling me Tersh."

She grinned at him, then gradually sobered before asking, "How did you feel about that?"

"Hated it, of course, but my protesting made it that much more fun for her. Soon other kids started, too, and after a while I got to like it. At least when someone yelled Tersh at a basketball game, there was no doubt I was the one being rooted for!"

"And did her big brother find a name to call her?"

"I confess to trying several, but none bothered her in the least, so I stopped." He chuckled.

"I'm afraid I wasn't imaginative enough, or so outrageously imaginative that the joke was on me."

Her fingers had worked their way between his as they followed the others onto the porch, and her cheek rested for a moment against his shoulder. "I do love you, Raymond John Hawkins, the Third, and let me assure you that I have no doubts about your being imaginative enough to fill every one of my dreams!"

They barely made it through the front door and into the hallway before she was in his arms again, and he was kissing her. "I love you more than I knew it was possible to love."

At the restaurant, Michael's autocratic demand for Denise to sit next to him was honored, and Jana relinquished her position on the other side of him to his newly introduced grandpa. "On condition that you won't sue me should you end up with berry handprints on your jacket or milk on your trousers," Jana said to Ray's father.

He raised his right hand as solemnly as though taking a courtroom oath. "I promise to hold myself, alone, accountable for any such mishap." As he took his seat, he commented in a loud aside to his son, "Be on guard, Ray. You've got yourself one smart woman!"

Jana felt warmed and accepted by this family, especially as Ray's arm came around her shoulders, his hand cupping her shoulder. "I certainly did get myself one smart and wonderful woman, Dad, for which I'll be eternally grateful."

George was the quietest person at the table, but Jana could tell by the sparkle in his eyes and his obviously following the give-and-take and banter of the rest of them that he was enjoying himself. Near the end of the meal, she asked, "How did someone as quiet as you ever get in this exuberant family?"

He laughed. "It was a case of her having to marry me, or someone like me. They need *some*-one willing to listen to all of them."

His wife pretend-punched his upper arm. "That's unkind, George!" But then, her eyes bright with laughter, she added, "Although partly true, of course—in addition to the fact that I was, and am, crazy in love with the guy."

Crazy in love. Jana looked at Ray, sitting beside her, and smiled. Yes, she could tell him that. "That's the way I feel about you, too, Ray."

He leaned over and kissed her on the lips, and

she kissed him back. She didn't look around to see how many other diners might be watching; she'd have kissed him just as freely on this pre-wedding night if this were the church or the administration building at the college or anywhere.

This is the man I'm marrying tomorrow, and I don't care if the whole world knows how much I love him!

Tomorrow. The lump in Ray's throat didn't go away with a sip of water or a cup of coffee. He'd been sitting next to the woman he loved, the woman he was about to marry—Jana, so trusting, so dear, so everything he wanted in a wife.

His family was pleased—he could easily tell that—and here he sat with their happy, contented conversation swirling around him, yet suddenly, mystifyingly, he found himself wondering if he could ever live up to the responsibilities he'd been so eager to take on.

Tomorrow.

What if he couldn't make or keep her happy? What if he were the unhappy one? She'd made it clear that she expected her marriage to last forever, but what if it didn't? He already loved little Michael like a son, yet what did he actually know of having a son?

Did all men go through times like this on the eve of their weddings, wondering about the future—wondering about all kinds of what-if's? Did Jana have some of these doubts, as well? If so, she'd covered them, but then he'd probably hid his concerns, too.

Let's look at this rationally, he told himself. *I didn't have these worries until tonight—not much, anyway. So I'm telling myself that I simply have pre-wedding jitters—and anyone should be entitled to those.*

Chapter Twelve

Everyone was talking, visiting and laughing, with no one in a hurry to leave. They dawdled over their meal, their decision-making as far as dessert was concerned, then the eating of it. Michael had been on his best behavior for the entire evening, but Ray figured Jana must have seen him yawning when she suggested, "Perhaps someone should be getting to bed, since he'll be having a big day tomorrow."

Gram nodded firmly. "I could use some sleep, too. If one of you would be kind enough to drive Michael and me home, I'll take care of that for both of us."

"Of course," Raymond said. "We'd be happy to do that."

At the same time, Jana was suggesting, "Perhaps it would be best to take me, instead. This will be my last night with him for a while, since we're flying to Vancouver right after the luncheon."

As was to be expected, that got offers from both Ray and his father—Michael siding with his mother's proposal once he realized what it was. Walking her to the door from the car perhaps fifteen minutes later, Ray asked, "Everything okay, Jana?"

"Very much so, but it struck me there at the table that tomorrow's the first time I will ever have left Michael for more than a day, and I would like to tuck him in tonight."

He thought she'd seemed hesitant about saying that and about to explain, but he touched her lips with the tip of his index finger. "It's all right, sweetheart. I certainly understand your having a bit of trepidation right before getting married."

"You, too?"

He grinned somewhat sheepishly. "Guilty as charged."

She looked concerned. "If you don't want to…"

He stopped her with another kiss. "I do want

to, Jana, I really do. It's just—this is the most monumental step I've ever made, and my analytical mind's so used to studying all sides of every decision that it keeps putting thoughts into my mind.''

"You're sure you do want to marry me?''

"Positive! And how about you? Are you sure you want to go through with this?''

"I, too, am positive.'' But then she confessed, with a smile, "Even though I'm having an occasional butterfly in my stomach.''

"Still have 'em?''

"A few, not many, and those are mostly beautiful, exotic ones. I do want, more than anything else in the world, to be your wife.''

Jana had permitted Michael to choose an extra book for bedtime reading, but he barely stayed awake for the end of it. They'd already prayed together, and tonight he added a new one. "Thanks for my new buddy. I like Aunt Denise and I'm glad she came to see me.''

I must remember to tell Denise that, Jana thought, then smiled ruefully, wondering if she'd be remembering much of anything tomorrow other than that it was her wedding day—that after noon tomorrow she would no longer be Jana Jenson, the unmarried mother of Michael. She would be Jana Hawkins, Mrs. Ray Hawkins, the wife of Professor Raymond John Hawkins, the Third.

No matter which way she said her name-to-be, it rolled through her mind beautifully, musically. And yet that last one did awaken a few fluttering butterflies. It's true she was aware of the social niceties of the country club set, but what of the academic community?

She'd mentioned her concerns, but Ray assured her she'd do fine, that he would help her get to know the people and be right there with and for her.

Am I insane thinking I can really be a helpmate, a true companion and helper for this man I love? You know, God, that I desire that more than anything. Please be with me, be with us tomorrow and on our honeymoon as we ride that train through western Canada and even more when we get back home.

There were many other thoughts and prayers as she prepared for bed and after she was already there. Gram returned to the house and came upstairs. ''Barb's not home yet, but I'm ready to call it a day, too," she told Jana, but did sit on the edge of the bed to talk for a few minutes.

"I just want to tell you again, Jana, what a fine woman you've become. I think back just four years, to when you came to me—how scared you were, how almost hopeless."

"I'd left everyone and everything I'd ever known and came with Grandma's minister to a strange town and a strange house. God was so very good in bringing me to you. After even a few days you were no longer a stranger. You were *Gram*."

The older woman's smile was a bit tremulous. "I didn't know what to expect, either. AnnaMae, Kate and Ricki were already here, and I just about had my hands full with GED studies in addition to all their other adjustments, and then there was you, and Barb, both in high school."

"I don't know how you did it, Gram, I really don't."

"When I look back on those first months, I marvel that we made it. There was so much I didn't know how to handle, and even those times when I thought I was doing things right, it didn't always work out that way."

"But you didn't give up on us, even when I

shoplifted that little infant dress so Barb's dear little dead baby would have something pretty to wear.''

"Oh, Jana...and I wasn't here to help with any of that!''

Jana recognized the pain Gram was going through, remembering being in the hospital with a broken hip. "But I learned so much from that experience—about myself, true, but also about so many truly good, wonderful people, like Vanessa, Rob, Gin and so many others who were willing to go out on a limb for me!''

"The thing is,'' Gram said as her hand reached to smooth Jana's hair from her forehead, "you were willing to learn from experiences, you were willing to make the effort to fit in here and do your part, to work at making it possible for all of you to have your babies.''

"Even if we weren't willing to give them up—'' her smile was a bit tremulous "—according to the plan.''

"By the time you four had your babies, that plan was obsolete—your keeping them was right for you. You'd grown enough and were stable enough that the original idea was wrong, and we all knew it!''

Gram stood up, obviously preparing to go to her room. "I'm very proud of all of you and I couldn't love you more, Jana, if you were my very own daughter or granddaughter. But now, dear, it's time for you to close your eyes and get some sleep. You have a big day coming up."

And, surprisingly, Jana did sleep—perhaps not as soundly and certainly not quite as long as she'd hoped, but she was pleased when she looked at the clock to find it was nearly five-thirty. She moved to the comfortable rocker by the window to read her devotional book and look up the scripture references, then to pray. She had her shower and was the first downstairs to start the coffee and heat water for tea.

Barb wandered in, still wearing her terry robe. Pouring coffee for herself, she asked, "Have a good time with your almost-in-laws last night?"

"Very good. I like Ray's family, and so does Michael. They're full of fun, especially his sister, and they all seem to love one another and don't take life more seriously than necessary."

"That's great. I have no idea how much contact you'll have with them, but their being able to see the humor of situations should help relationships," Barb said.

"Good morning, girls." Gram came in and headed for the kitchen counter. "Waffles or pancakes this morning—which would you prefer?"

"Let's let the bride make this important decision," Barb suggested. "After all, this is her day."

"I choose waffles, then."

Gram opened one of the lower cupboards and brought out the well-used waffle iron, set it on the countertop and plugged it in before preparing the batter. She was lifting the lid to remove the first waffles when Michael arrived. "Oh, Gram! Waffles! I love waffles. Can I put maple syrup and butter on mine?"

"I don't see why not, Michael," she said, placing one of the squares on his plate.

"I want more than one."

"Oh, I certainly do hope so. My goodness, with you growing so fast, you certainly need more than one. And your mama and aunt and I will each have one of these first ones, too, just like you, and then we'll each have another of the next ones and the next. That way, we'll all get to eat while they're good and warm."

"Yeah, while good and warm," he repeated.

It was all Jana could do to keep from putting

in words of wisdom or encouragement, but she kept silent. Gram and Barb would be responsible for her son the two weeks she'd be gone, so it was best for him to be listening to Gram this morning.

She found herself blinking rapidly and swallowing hard as it hit her again that she'd be away from her little one for fourteen days instead of only hours, as had been true all his life. Maybe she should have said that seeing Canada's western area by train and stopping at a number of historical and railroad sites was just a little too ambitious, that she shouldn't be away that long.

But she had not and would not. Michael was in the best of hands, and his mother would be in frequent phone contact. And furthermore, all his friends and loved ones would be right here with him.

All but his mother and his by then newly pronounced father.

Jana managed to eat only one waffle and a banana, along with her tea. It was less than usual, but nobody mentioned that, and she was able to sit there with her son and Gram and Barb as they ate.

And the hands of the clock seemed to be going around faster than ever before.

With the exception of those items that would be in her garment bag, most of the clothing she planned to take was already in the open suitcases on the floor beside her dresser. She'd considered moving things to the apartment before she got married, then changed her mind when learning that Denise and George would be staying there.

She was aware of all kinds of books on bridal etiquette, shelves of them in stores and libraries, but she'd not checked to see what others thought about when to move in to one's groom's apartment. Living this close to Gram and being free of college study until fall, she'd have plenty of opportunity to transfer Michael's and her things.

Moving out of Gram's! Moving from one home to another! The only time in her life she'd done this was when she came to Gram's, and what a change that had been.

But this time she was moving because of love.

She stopped short, standing in the middle of her bedroom, realizing for the first time that her previous move, too, had been for love, though she hadn't known to call it such. For that matter, she'd not fully recognized why she'd so adamantly refused to have the abortion. She already loved Michael before she'd seen him or knew if he was a boy or a girl, or held him in her arms, or anything.

She remembered one of her pastor's recent sermons, when he stressed that God knows each person intimately even before that infant is born, and that He loves each one, and wants all of them in His family.

Wow, I'm in a philosophical mood this morning! She smiled a little and went to Michael's chest of drawers to take out the new clothing for him to wear today.

She'd almost expected clouds of butterflies when walking down the staircase for the last time as an unmarried woman, but Ray was waiting for her in the hallway, looking incredibly handsome, so loving, so welcoming. For a moment that seemed like a strange word for her mind to come up with, but it was the right one.

He was wearing a new, perfectly tailored dark blue suit and white shirt, and had on the silk tie she'd purchased last week and given to him. But it was his eyes and his face that filled her with joy, the warmth and love showing clearly there, as well as in his extended arms and his hands, palms up, waiting for hers to be placed within his keeping.

"You are so beautiful." His voice was little more than a whisper. "And I love you very much."

She was in his arms. "And I'm indescribably happy to be marrying you today."

Barb was coming down the steps behind her, carrying the large suitcase and garment bag Jana had left in her room. "You two are making me jealous."

Jana started to release herself from the hug. "Your turn will come, my special friend. Your turn will come."

An overly dramatic sigh accompanied Barb's, "Oh, I do hope so!" And she grinned at them as she set the luggage near the front door.

Ray and Jana walked together to the kitchen. "I expect to sit through church all right, Gram," he told her, "but getting through Sunday school before that this morning may be a major test of my ability to keep my mind on a lesson."

"Why doesn't that surprise me?" Gram asked, coming to hug him. "I'm sure God will understand if your mind wanders, but you'll undoubtedly be teased by your class members should your responses be too far off the subject.''

''I'll try to remember that.''

There was activity at the front door, and Michael was squealing with happiness as he ran toward it, shouting, ''Aunt Denise is here, 'n' Grandpa and Grandma and Uncle George!''

Denise came hurrying in, the others following. ''How's my special buddy this morning?'' she greeted, picking up the child and holding him close.

His arms were around her neck and he kissed her. ''*We're* gettin' married this morning.''

Jana's hand squeezed Ray's tightly, and her quick glance met his as he agreed, ''Yes, we are. He's exactly right.''

She was almost overwhelmed by the generous nature, the goodness of this man. ''Thank you, Ray.''

He apparently understood.

Ray's family went with them to Karlyn's class, and Jana wondered if that's why everyone seemed to be on especially good behavior. Oh, there was joking and teasing at first, but everyone settled down as Karlyn, Gram's granddaughter, who was part of this large circle of students, began the lesson.

"One of the best things about being the teacher is that I have almost unlimited freedom as to how I choose to teach a particular lesson. And, for today, I'm assuming one more freedom, that of changing the order of which Bible lesson to teach.

"For our visitors, let me say that we've been in the book of First Corinthians for the past month or so. I am temporarily skipping a couple of chapters to bring us to the thirteenth one—especially the last verse, where Paul writes that three things abound in the Christian life—faith, hope and love, and the greatest of these is love."

She briefly reviewed a few things about Corinth and about Paul, the great apostle missionary whose letters have been so important for almost two millennia. She was able to draw the students into a discussion concerning different kinds of love before focusing on one of them.

Reaching down to the side of her chair, she brought up a large white plastic bag as she said, "Jana and Ray, the members of your class have taken on a project about which I believe you know nothing."

She slid from that bag what looked like a large white leather-bound book. "You may already have one of these for wedding pictures, but *this* one is something I believe you will treasure almost as much.

"As you see," she said, turning it around, "the title of your book is *The Greatest of These Is Love,* the calligraphy for which was done by Gin Redding. The people you see in this circle have asked each individual in the church over the age of fourteen—and a few younger ones also wished to be included—to write something about love, something she or he would like to share with you. In some cases this is a reminiscence of something in their past, and I'll confess that some of these, which I couldn't resist reading as I put this together, brought tears to my eyes.

"There are also helpful hints, some given by couples who've celebrated forty, fifty, sixty or more years together—several appreciably more than that. These are of both interest and value.

"In the reading of these words, you may come to love many of our people even more and understand some of them better—but most of all, we pray that this volume, a labor of love, will let you know how much we all do appreciate and love you.

"We pray both of you will have a blessed marriage that will last all of your lives, and that you will fully realize that the greatest of blessings, as Paul wrote, is truly love."

Jana looked around at these people who had been so instrumental in helping her to learn to trust and to love again, and had been with her along her spiritual journey. She wanted to say something like that, to share what they meant to her, but wasn't sure she could.

She walked over to receive the book from Karlyn and held it close. "Truly, the greatest of these is love," she said. "I thank you from the bottom of my heart for being such good friends, such wonderful Christians.

"I hope that each of you has written in our book, but if there's anyone who hasn't yet done so, please do. I love you all, every one."

She could not go on.

The class was over, and many spoke to her and Ray and his family. "I don't know how you can be so calm," several told her, not sensing that she was getting less so by the minute, and others spoke of the uniqueness of having the wedding at the end of the morning worship service, which was soon to begin.

She was almost wishing she wasn't doing it this way. *But I'd probably be even more nervous if I were in a back room right now in a fancy white gown and train and veil and carrying a bouquet of orchids.*

Ray was beside her as they entered the front of the large sanctuary, and she gasped at seeing nearly every seat filled with not only church members, but friends she knew from school and town and some she'd met at the railroad meetings. There were also many she didn't know, probably friends or acquaintances of Ray's.

They crossed to the center aisle and went to the second row. Gram had Michael on her lap, and the other four of Gram's girls were in front with the three children. Ray's parents and his sister and her husband were also here.

She'd tried not to look around too much, but her glance had wandered along the aisle and returned to focus on one couple halfway back. Her feet suddenly stopped as she was entering the row, and Ray leaned close to whisper, "Are you okay?"

She swallowed hard, moved a step closer to

Gram and Michael and managed to get out two words. "My—parents!"

Ray sat beside her and held her hand between his, rubbing it. "You're sure?"

She nodded, but the suddenness of it made it seem almost unreal. She could do nothing about it, either. What should she be doing?

The choir was processing, singing a joyful hymn, and the pastor was bringing up the rear.

Jana saw all this, but everything still seemed almost hallucinatory. She'd been writing those letters for four long years. She had sent pictures. She had told them that she was getting married today.

And they were here!

They had not smiled but, with the shock of it, neither had she.

They had given no wave or anything.

Nor had she.

She wanted to rejoice that her prayers were answered, that they could once again be a family, but perhaps that wasn't true.

Why else would they be here, unannounced but present? With a shudder she recalled the scene from *Jane Eyre*, one of those old, old books of Gram's in the upper hallway bookcase, which she'd read shortly after coming to Sylvan Falls. Someone had deliberately gone to Jane's marriage to cause trouble—to be there when the preacher came to that often-asked question, did anyone have knowledge of any reason the wedding should not take place.

They couldn't be here for that, could they? They wouldn't be so cruel as to publicly humiliate her in that fashion, would they? *Oh, God, please...not that!*

She tried to focus on Pastor Harriman. He, too, was using I Corinthians 13 as the scripture for the service. But she found herself unable to keep her thoughts on what he was saying.

Michael wanted to sit on her lap, and Gram was telling him to stay with her, to not rumple Mama's pretty white suit and blouse. This was good advice, yet she longed to hold him in her arms, no matter what happened to the suit she'd shopped so long and hard to find.

Ray was still rubbing her hand, and she tried to smile at him but sensed he wasn't reassured. "Just pray, dear," she whispered. "Pray hard for all of us."

"I am, Jana. And I'll always be here."

That was what she needed to hear, but she recognized that she still had not conquered that old self-doubt. "I love you."

"I know. And I love you, too."

What will people think—us talking together like this during church as we're about to be married?

I've got to shape up. Help me, God, to be worthy of Ray. Help me to never shame him. Nor Michael. Nor Gram.

She forced herself to sit up straight. To sing the hymns. To look at the choir as they sang their anthem. To listen more closely to the message and prayer of the pastor.

By the time Pastor Harriman was well into the sermon, she was able to listen, realizing that he'd planned this especially for her and Ray and those here today. It was about love and caring, about God's ordaining marriage as the oneness of a loving man and a loving woman who chose to commit themselves to a faithful relationship so strong and so full of love that it was where they both desired to be for the rest of their lives.

He stated that this kind of relationship was the perfect growth medium in which children and family members could develop and help others grow to their full potential.

"Today we have with us many fine men and women who have dedicated their lives, their love, their families and their homes to Christ, and we thank God for each of these.

"And today we have many babies and children and young people who are the products of such homes, those places of such oneness of the parents that the children are well-rounded, secure individuals who have a good probability of raising the next generation in like fashion.

"And the marvelous, almost incredible part of this is that all men and women truly joined together in Christ are one."

That seemed to Jana like a good wrap-up for the sermon, and she was wondering just how he was going to lead into their marriage when he said, "I have the privilege of asking Jana Jenson and Raymond Hawkins to please come forward."

The minister was walking to the lower level as Ray, on his feet first, took her hand to help Jana to hers. She'd wondered what would happen if she were to trip or something awful like that, and a few minutes ago had fretted about what her parents might do, but she was now filled with the assurance that everything would be all right.

As she got to the aisle, preparing to turn and

move to the front of the church, she couldn't keep from glancing toward her parents. She saw tears running down her mother's cheeks, and her father was wiping his eyes, too. Without even thinking about it, she found herself smiling at them.

At my mother and father, whom I'd feared I would never see again, whom for a long time I never wanted to see again!

She and Ray took their places facing Pastor Harriman, who smiled at both of them before speaking to the congregation those traditional words, "Dearly beloved, we are gathered together here in the sight of God and in the presence of this congregation to join together this man and this woman in holy matrimony."

God's in His Heaven, all's right with the world. That line from Robert Browning flashed into her mind, making her feel warm and loved. *Yes, God, You really are—and it is.*

"It is not, therefore, to be entered into lightly or unadvisedly, but reverently, soberly and in the fear of God. So it is fitting that on this joyous occasion we first seek His divine blessing. Let us pray."

Jana prayed along with him, her silent thankfulness and supplications sincere. Then came their vows, first Ray's, then hers, and she answered with absolute truthfulness, "I will," when asked, "Jana, do you take this man to be your lawful wedded husband? And do you solemnly promise, before God and these witnesses, that you will love, honor and cherish him and that, forsaking all others for him alone, you will perform unto him all the duties that a wife owes to her husband until God, by death, shall separate you?"

This led into the giving and receiving of the plain gold rings they'd chosen together several weeks ago. And then the minister said, "Since it is your desire to take each other as wife and husband, please indicate that by joining your right hands and repeating after me in the presence of God and this congregation your marriage vows."

Again Ray went first, and then it was her turn to give those age-old words of commitment that with only slight variation had been promised millions of times before.

"I, Jana, take you, Raymond, to be my wedded husband, to have and to hold from this day forward, for better or worse, for richer or poorer, in health or in sickness, to love and to cherish as long as we both shall live, according to God's holy ordinance. To you I promise my faithfulness.''

"You have now pledged your love and your faithfulness to one another. I would remind you, however, that it is only in your day-by-day acceptance of the responsibilities as well as the joys of marriage that you can mature and help one another to grow in your love," the pastor told them.

She did not let go of Ray's hand as the pastor continued, "This is a wondrous new relationship—strong, yet all too easily broken, joyous, yet far too often troubled. It is your responsibility to strengthen one another and to strive always to heal the little hurts before they become big ones, and try to avoid or straighten out very soon those misunderstandings that can grow into weeds of jealousy or argumentation or hostility that can choke out the bloom of love.

"I would pray for you a whole garden of weed-free blessings, but we know there will always be some trials and difficulties. However, we also know that the Lord of love is always there to help you and sustain you if you will strive to do your part.

"Remember always...."

There was a rush of little feet coming toward them. Michael had evidently had enough of being left out of this wedding and had come to join them. Jana started to reach for his hand, but Ray leaned over to pick him up and hold him. The child looked over his new father's shoulder and said quite distinctly, "There's lots of people here today."

The minister smiled as he incorporated that thought. "There are, indeed, lots of people in your lives, but you have chosen one another to live with and to love in a special, God-given way. Treasure your friendships, but cherish one another. Share liking and love with those beyond your family, but always remember this marriage bond you have made today, and keep it sacred."

Jana saw him raise his hand to give them his blessing and Michael's arm rising as his little fingers reached up to touch those of the pastor, as though templed in prayer.

Neither Ray nor Jana had made any effort to stop that, and later, after their honeymoon, which proved to be everything they'd hoped for, when all the photographs had been carefully arranged in their wedding album, including those taken with their parents, that was the picture chosen to be enlarged and placed under the protective transparent plastic of the cover.

Beneath it, in Ray's bold, firm script, were written Michael's words spoken to Denise that morning. "WE'RE GETTIN' MARRIED THIS MORNING!"

And their married life, their family life, was very, very good.

* * * * *

Dear Reader,

How pleased I am that you're with us once again in Sylvan Falls, Pennsylvania, the home of Gram McHenry. You met her and her extended family in *A Family for Andi*, when that title character came from a distance to "find her roots." We came together again in *A Special Kind of Family*, after Gram had taken into her home pregnant girls who planned to give up their babies for adoption as soon as they were born. However, Vanessa, her granddaughter, reluctantly took over these responsibilities when Gram was hospitalized.

In *A Family for Jana*, you've gotten to know this young woman who tries to juggle everything—mothering her own three-year-old, helping with other children, being a college junior—and now involved in an unlikely romance.

But isn't life like that? We think we've reached the limit of what we can handle—only to find more's required. It is often in those times, however, with God giving us the strength to go on, that we do much of our essential growing.

I am blessed to be living just outside a relatively small town in which people live and love and act much like those in Sylvan Falls. For that matter, my husband (my own real-life hero) loves trains as much as Ray does— and the church, schools, libraries, etc., are as important to us as to Gram, Jana, Andi, Vanessa and all the rest.

Eileen Berger